THE MOON TOUCHED CHRONICLES

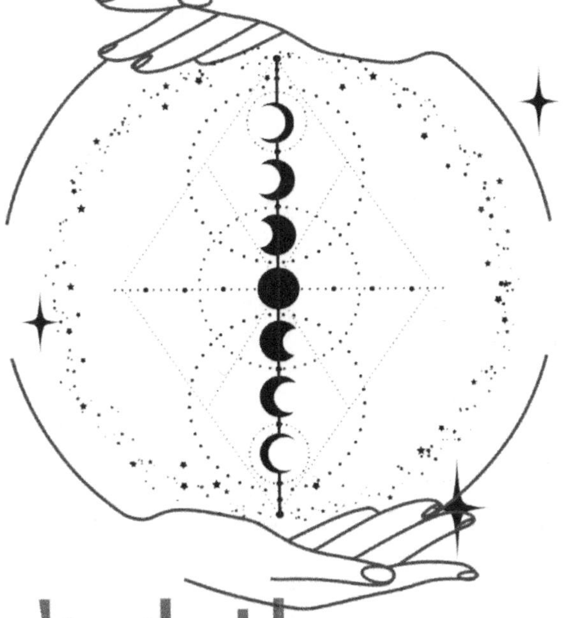

Nighthowl

RUBY ELLIS

For the warriors who wear their scars on and under their skin. Your strength shines bright—even through your darkest days.

Content Warning

This book contains strong language, sexually explicit scenes, discussions of sexual assault, drugging, violence, self-harm, panic attacks, kidnapping, trafficking, child neglect, societal infertility, pregnancy, childbirth, and loss.

Ramsey is a survivor. While her experiences are discussed and shown via nightmares, the assault happened prior to her arriving in this world and is not at the hands of our MMC. Griffin is a supportive partner who loves Ramsey through her healing.

Table of Contents

Chapter One

Everything around me is dirty.

My clothes? Dirty.

The floor? Dirty.

My skin? Dirty.

Their hands on me? Dirty.

Hunger gnaws at my stomach as I struggle to keep my eyes open. It used to be a familiar feeling—starvation—but it has been years since I last endured the pain. My eyes drift closed and I am taken back to those days early in my life. Days and nights when I rationed the food that I took from school so that my sisters could eat.

When their *whimpers and cries were the ones that I heard at night instead of the noises that surround me now.*

I sit up, shaken back to the very real Hell that I am living in now, and try to breathe.

The air that I pull into my lungs is thick with cigarette smoke and the smell of unwashed bodies. I am alone in my cell. Empty. Just the shell of the person I once was as company. There were others, but they are gone now. I don't know where they went but I could hear their cries as they were taken. My sisters cried when they were taken from me too—but I got them back.

The women from the cell won't be coming back.

Only men.

The men visit me in my cell. Sometimes they take me to another room. But I always return to my cell after.

I don't know why they keep me. I wish they wouldn't. I can find my sisters in another life. This one isn't worth living anymore.

No.

If I allow myself to think like that, I will never make it out of here alive. I need to focus. I need water. I need to get clean.

I need to wash this place from my soul.

The walls are closing in around me. It is suffocating. I need to breathe but I cannot get air.

Footsteps.

No. No no no! I make myself small. I hide in the corner. Please keep walking. Please choose someone else.

The footsteps stop outside my cell. No! Please no! I am still dirty!

"Wake up, Angel." The voice is soft and calm. It pulls me from my nightmare.

I look around, unsure as to where I am. The room slowly comes into focus, but the decorated walls are unfamiliar.

I can feel tears running down my face and my throat is burning from screaming in my cell without water.

"You are safe," the voice says. I turn towards the sound and startle when I see a man kneeling by my bed. A bed. I'm not in the cell. I am not in that Hell where monsters feed off of my body as they eat away at my soul.

Not a man. Griffin.

It was just a dream. I let out a relieved breath.

"What are you doing in here?" I ask as I quickly smooth my hair out of my face. I didn't mean for my tone to sound so harsh, but I don't like that he saw me like this. Terrified. Shaking. Weak.

Griffin stays kneeling but backs away from me. His blue eyes turned navy in the darkness of night. "I was in the library," he explains, nodding to the wall behind the headboard of my bed. "You were yelling in your sleep. I apologize for startling you." I cannot read the look that flashes in his eyes before he forces them back into a quiet calm. Was it pity? Fear?

"Oh." Embarrassment makes my cheeks heat. "Well, thank you for waking me. It was just a bad dream." I pull my knees up to my chest and hide my face from his view. He reaches out to touch me but pulls his hand back away before he makes contact.

"Do you want to talk about it?" His voice is like a balm to my frayed edges. I don't know why he has this effect on me. I don't feel safe around any man. Not anymore. But Griffin brings me comfort. It doesn't make any sense. I don't even know him but I have to stop myself from reaching out and running my hands through his hair. He keeps it cut shorter than most males that I have seen in this world. Every time that I have seen him his hair is slightly mussed, like he often runs his hands through it while he is thinking or reading. I desperately want to know if it is as soft as it looks.

Realizing that he asked me a question, I shake my head. I don't want to ever talk about it. I have been having the same nightmares since I arrived in this world. Estelle, Griffin's aunt, tried to get me to open up about it once, but I couldn't. If they knew…No. They cannot know. They would look at me differently. They would see me how I see myself. Broken. Stained.

Logically, I understand that what happened to me was not my fault. I should be able to talk about it. I probably *need* to talk about it. But I can't. Not yet. Maybe not ever.

"Is there anything that I can get you?" He hands me a cup of water, anticipating my needs before I can voice them. My hands are shaking so bad that I almost spill the water as I lift it to my mouth. But he does not comment on it. He simply reaches out to steady the cup with his own grip.

I shake my head again. "It was just a bad dream. I'm okay now." I know that he can hear the lie for what it is, but he gets up and heads towards the door anyway.

Turning back towards me before he leaves the room, I can tell that he is trying to decide if he should leave or stay. "Are you sure that you are okay?" he asks one more time. *Stay,* my inner voice pleads, but I nod and try to smile. It doesn't quite work but it is the best that I can offer him right now.

As soon as he leaves, I get out of bed and start the bath. I need to get clean. I scrub my skin until it is almost raw and then get dressed again for bed. Rowan had brought me some of her clothes, but I am wearing one of Griffin's shirts. I know that it is his because it smells like him. It brings me comfort even though it shouldn't. He smells like home in a way that I have never been able to find before.

I should wrap my hair in a towel or braid it out of my face, but I am too exhausted, so I let my long strands soak through the shoulders of my borrowed shirt. He was only in here for a few minutes, but I am overwhelmed by the kindness that he showed me—the support that he has shown me from the very start. I'm not sure if I even deserve it. I certainly didn't do anything to warrant it from him. But he offers it anyway.

Inhaling his spicy scent, I pull the blankets up over my head and cry myself back to sleep.

Chapter Two

Griffin

I can hear her crying through the door. I can scent the saltiness of her tears. My wolf is screaming at me to go and hold her. To make her feel better—but she is not comfortable with me yet. So, I sit outside her door. I will protect her from a distance. I will stay out in the hall and will wake her again if her nightmare returns. Just like I have done every night since she arrived.

There is not much that I know about my Mate. She is breathtaking. Her eyes are an alluring shade of green and her hair is dark like chocolate. She looks thin, too thin, but I will make sure that she eats.

I look down at the moon markings that decorate my hands. A physical reminder of what she is to me. What we are to each other. Moon Touched. Something I had only read about before my brother showed up with a Mate and the same markings decorating his chest.

Ramsey used an incredible amount of magic to heal Rowan and her babies. Magic that heals.

My Mate might not want my help with her nightmares, she definitely is not comfortable enough to tell me about them, but I will find answers for her about her powers.

We have a few weeks until the full moon—which means I have a few weeks to convince her to bond with me. Technically, we could wait longer, but she is so fragile in this world without the bond. I have this overwhelming *need* to protect her—to keep her safe. It is stronger than anything I have ever felt before. And, I know that it is probably due to our True Mate pairing, but I also know, deep down in my bones, that she has not been protected in the past. Something terrified her enough that it still follows her into her dreams. Hopefully, with time, she will feel comfortable enough to let me care for her in the way she deserves.

I will be patient. She is mine and I am hers. Our souls are tied together regardless of whether we do the ceremony or not. I will do everything I can to show her that she can trust me.

I listen closely until her cries have stopped and her breathing has evened out. She must have fallen back asleep. I let out a deep breath and shift into my wolf, settling in for the night in my spot against her door.

She has been here for a couple of days but she has yet to leave her room. My Aunt Estelle delivers her food and Rowan has checked in on her—but she spends most of her time in fitful sleep. Estelle had mentioned that Ramsey had trouble sleeping, but it makes my skin itch with a need to provide comfort. She said that Ramsey will come out when she is ready and I have to hope that Estelle is right.

But I feel unsettled.

So, I wait outside her door. I wake her from her nightmares. And I hope that one day she will let me be more.

I am woken up the next morning when Ramsey's door is pulled open, causing my large wolf body to splat on the ground at her feet. She looks down and lets out a gasp, holding her hand to her heart.

"I am never going to get used to this," she mumbles to herself.

I forget to breathe as I look up at her, hair tangled from sleep with the sun shining in behind her. She is glowing. Fucking beautiful. I don't think I will ever get used to this either.

Readying myself to shift, I pause when she crouches down to pet my head. "You are pretty adorable like this, though," she adds. I chuff out a laugh. Adorable. I have been called many things, but adorable is not what most people think when they see my massive wolf.

She seems more comfortable with me like this than she did last night, so I decided to stay in this form. I follow Ramsey as she makes her way towards the kitchen. It is still early and I doubt War and Rowan will be leaving their bed any time soon. Bade has not returned from his mission yet, though he should be sending an update soon.

Ramsey stops in the hall, unsure of which direction to go. I slowly walk closer and lower my head so that it is under her hand and direct her towards the kitchen and dining room. I need to make sure that she eats this morning. The trays that Estelle delivers to her go mostly untouched.

Feeling more comfortable staring at her while I am in this form, I let myself take a long look. She is wearing one of my shirts—though it is big enough to be a dress on her. I know that Rowan brought her some clothes but a primal part of me loves that she chose my shirt instead. Her mossy green eyes are more vibrant in the morning light than they were last night. Her lash lines are slightly pinked, telling of the tears she let fall last night after I left her room. Even with the skin under her eyes being sunken in from lack of sleep, she is the most stunning creature I have ever laid eyes on.

I know that this is all too much for her to process all at once, but there is no way that she doesn't feel the pull of our souls. If I am honest with myself, I will admit that I have been feeling a pull for months. Probably since she first appeared in this world. But it was mild and I was so busy that I did not think much of it at the time. Now that we have met, it is impossible to ignore. My chest aches with the need to be close to her.

I bring Ramsey into the dining room, where my father is eating his breakfast. She pauses when she sees him, her hand moving from my head to her chest as she starts to back away, her breathing becoming choppy. I quickly place myself between them and walk with her as she backs out of the room.

My father remains still, glancing up with only his eyes as he sees our entrance and sudden exit from the room.

"Is she okay?" my father asks mentally.

"I'm not sure. I will figure it out."

Once she is fully out of the room, I let the door close behind us and she slides down the wall, bringing her knees up to her chest. I sit beside her and nudge her arm with my nose. I do not want to startle her out by shifting right now, but I need her to know that I am here for her.

She doesn't hesitate as she pulls me into a hug and buries her face into my fur.

"I'm sorry that I am broken," she says quietly. I whimper, not liking that she thinks that of herself. She could never be anything other than perfect in my eyes.

Estelle calmly walks up to us, placing a gentle hand on Ramsey's shoulder. It has been years since Estelle has been to the lodge. She looks so much like my mother, it always takes me a moment to remember who she isn't.

"Are you okay, dear?" Estelle asks Ramsey. I do not have all of the details from before Ramsey arrived at the lodge, but I know that she appeared in my territory and was nursed back to health by Estelle before they made the long journey here. It took them longer to travel here because they needed to stay in the shadows. There were far too many of Dreena's sympathizers in my territory.

I will forever be grateful to Estelle for keeping my Mate safe and bringing her to me—even if she did not know that it was what she was doing at the time. They heard rumblings about a human witch and Ramsey was certain that she would find at least one of her sisters here. She was right. Smart girl.

"I couldn't...there was a man in there," Ramsey tells Estelle in a whisper. Estelle nods, understanding more than I do right now.

"Would you like me to go in with you or should I make you a plate and bring it out? Either way, you need to eat."

After thinking over the options, Ramsey asks Estelle to bring her a plate, her cheeks flushing red with embarrassment. I nudge her neck with my nose, hoping she understands that I will help make everything okay. Even if I do not yet understand what is troubling her.

Estelle returns moments later with two plates of food, completely loaded with a little bit of everything.

"Thank you," I thank her mentally.

"Of course, Alpha," she replies out loud. Ramsey looks between us, probably wondering what just happened.

I follow Ramsey back to her room, laying down at her feet while she eats.

"Are you going to stay wolfy?" she asks me after picking at some of the food on her plate.

Not wanting to freak her out, I leave the room to shift and put on some pants. When I return, she offers me a small smile. It still does not reach her eyes, but it is a little brighter than the smile she gave me last night. Progress.

"How are you feeling this morning?" I ask.

"I'm okay," she replies. "I'm sorry that I woke you up again last night."

"You didn't," I assure her. "I was still awake in the library. I am trying to find a passage that I read a while ago about moon magic. Originally, it was to help War and Ro, but it seems we need the information for us too."

Ramsey nods and slowly munches on a piece of sausage but doesn't say anything else.

"Are you okay with me being here? I can shift back if it makes you more comfortable."

"No, that's okay. You can be here. I, um, sometimes get nervous around men. It's kind of...it's new for me. But you don't make me feel that way," she says quietly.

My mind goes wild, thinking of the reasons why she would feel uncomfortable around men. I know that someone hurt her and I will do everything that I can to make sure she knows she is safe.

"The man at breakfast was my father, Lycus," I tell her. "Do you remember him from when you first arrived? I know that there was a lot going on at that time." Ramsey gives a slight nod. "You are safe with him. Just like you will always be safe with me and my brothers. But, if it would make you feel better, I can be with you whenever you need. Either like this or as a wolf."

She sets down her fork but continues looking at her plate instead of meeting my gaze. "I was so focused on Ro that I blocked everything and everyone else out. I had to. It was the only way that I could make myself walk into that room filled with wolves and strangers. That is going to take some getting used to. The whole wolf thing, I mean. I have been in this world for a few months, but I only saw Estelle shift once. She told me about this world, what I should expect, but it is different seeing it. When we traveled, we made sure that we didn't come in contact with anyone. We didn't know who we could trust."

"Rowan has shared a little bit about the world that you came from. It was an adjustment for her too—though it seems like she is comfortable now."

Ramsey nods. "She told me that her Mate is Warrick...War? Is he your brother?"

"Yes. We are triplets, actually. Our other brother Bade runs our military and he is dealing with an issue at the moment."

"The witch hunters?"

I chuckle softly. I hadn't heard that term before but it was fitting. "Yes. Not everyone is happy about War finding his True Mate in a non-wolf shifter. A woman named Dreena became jealous and started a bit of a rebellion."

"Is that who attacked Rowan?"

"No. That was Zuri. She was one of Dreena's supporters. She is gone now, though. My father ripped out her throat when she stabbed Rowan."

Ramsey gasped.

"I'm sorry," I say instantly, keeping my tone soft as I internally berate myself. "I didn't mean for my words to be so harsh. You do not need to fear my father. His wolf was trying to protect Rowan and her babies."

"I still can't believe that she is pregnant. She never even talked about wanting kids back home."

"To be honest, I'm not sure there was much thought of it here either. She went into heat during their bonding ceremony and her magic promotes healthy fertility. I do not think anything could have stopped it from happening. They are very happy though."

"She has magic too?"

"Yes. I can tell you all about it, but I do not want to overwhelm you. Please let me know if it is too much, okay?"

"I promise," she says, taking another bite of her food. "I do better when I have all of the facts. I feel steadier."

I nod my understanding. I like knowing the facts too. "As wolf-shifters, we believe that we were given life by The Mother. Many years ago, when the First Wolf roamed, he felt lonely and went to The Mother asking for a Mate. She gave him his, well I guess you could call it his human half. When he still felt there was something missing, he went back to The Mother and she granted him his True Mate—the owner of part of his soul. War and Rowan are True Mates. They each hold a part of the other's soul."

"And you think that is what we are?" she asks quietly.

"I know that we are True Mates."

She nods but does not say anything else. I do not want to inundate her with information, so I just sit quietly while she processes.

"Would you like some of this food?" she asks me after a while. "There is too much for just me to eat."

"I will eat when you are full. I need to make sure that you get enough."

"Why?"

Because I need to make sure that your every possible need and desire are met before taking anything for myself. I know she has not been eating much since she arrived. But that would be too much for her to hear right now. "It is just part of my instincts," I say instead. "Some of our behaviors are a bit more wolf than man in this world."

She accepts my vague answer, continuing to eat until she is full and then passes her plate over to me. I give her a smile before eating the rest of the food off of her plate.

"War and Rowan do not usually emerge from their love nest until later in the morning. With the attack, War has been feeling extra...attached. Would you like to join me for a walk in the garden? Or I could show you around the lodge."

"I would like that," she says. "Just let me get cleaned up first."

I walk over to her wardrobe and pull out one of my shirts to pull over my head. Then I wait for her outside her door. A few minutes later, Ramsey pops her head out the door.

"Is there any way you can find me a more modest dress or shirt? I'm not comfortable wearing what Rowan brought me. I did not realize everything was so revealing."

"Oh, of course. I will be right back, Angel."

Not wanting her to have to wait too long, I run down the hall to enter War's quarters.

"Stop whatever you are doing—I am coming in."

I open his door, shielding my eyes just in case I did not give them enough time. I am not all that concerned with nudity, but I know that Rowan is and I do not need War's possessive ass growling at me.

Rowan giggles at me. "It's okay, Griffin. We are just eating some breakfast in bed. Is there something that you need?"

Turning to look at them, I am slightly surprised to see that they are, in fact, just eating breakfast in bed.

"Ramsey asked if I could find something for her to wear that is more modest than what you brought her. I was thinking maybe one of your dresses that covers a bit more?"

"Of course, she can have anything that she wants. I didn't really think too much of it when I brought her some clothes last night. I just grabbed some things that don't fit me at the moment. Is she okay? She has never really been shy about her body before."

19

I rummage through their wardrobe to grab a few options. "I think that she is still adjusting to life here."

I do not tell her that Ramsey is having nightmares or that she is uncomfortable around men. For some reason, it feels like it would be betraying the trust that she has given me so far.

"Thanks for these," I say on my way out. "I will have the clothier come this week so she can have some things made." I leave the room and quickly return to my Mate.

Chapter Three

Ramsey

"This garden is beautiful," I say, gently lifting a delicate bloom with my hand. After he returned with a dress for me to wear, Griffin gave me a tour of the lodge and now, we have made our way outside to enjoy some sun. "I bet Rowan loves it out here. She has always had such a green thumb."

Griffin snorts. "She actually made this all happen with her magic. At first, it was by accident. All of those vines that you see climbing the walls and surrounding that balcony sprung up whenever she, um, found pleasure." Griffin's cheeks turn pink as he points out the outer wall of the lodge that has erupted with life.

I chuckle. "Poor girl was always too shy to bring a guy home back in New York but here plants broadcast her orgasms to the world."

"It is hard to stay shy when your Mate is openly talking about your magic pussy at the dinner table," he tacks on.

I double over laughing. I look up to see Griffin smiling wide at me, a soft look in his eyes.

"You have a beautiful laugh, Angel." Griffin reaches out to tuck a stray piece of hair behind my ear.

I feel my cheeks blush and force myself to stay steady as his fingers lightly brush against my skin. He is so gentle with me, but the look in his eyes holds so much heat, I feel like I could combust if I stare at him too long.

After a moment of simply existing in the shared breath between us, we walk into the center of the garden where a table has been set up for lunch. My stomach chooses that moment to grumble.

"We usually have lunch out here as a family, but if you are not feeling up to it, we can eat somewhere else," he offers. He has not asked me to explain my behavior this morning at breakfast. I am nervous to be around others, but if Rowan and Estelle are here, I think I will be okay.

"I would like to try," I say, looking at the six place settings. "But can I sit between you and Rowan, with Estelle across from me?"

He doesn't even blink at my strange request. "Of course," he says with a smile.

"And if I need to escape..."

Griffin cautiously reaches out, tipping my chin back up to look in his eyes. "If you need to escape, I will take you wherever you feel safest. No questions asked."

I get lost in the pools of his eyes, knowing with absolute certainty that he is telling me the truth. But can I trust him with mine?

The others make their way into the garden a few minutes later. Griffin must have done that mind communication thing because everyone sat down in their designated places without me needing to say anything. Rowan greeted me with a hug and we held each other a little extra. It was so hard being away from her for so long, worrying about what she had gone through or where she ended up. Now that I know we are both here, I know that Reese must be here too. We need to find her.

Everyone chats around me, asking me a few questions but mostly just having a normal family discussion. Rowan is beyond comfortable with these people. She has made this world her home and I hope that

I will be able to feel the same one day. She shares that she is reading Griffin's mom's journal from when she was pregnant with him, War, and Bade. I look at Estelle and Lycus, Griffin's father, and see tears in their eyes despite the smiles on their faces.

Estelle told me that her twin sister, Helen, died in childbirth when the boys were young. I know that it is hard for her to be at the lodge, and I am forever grateful that she helped me get here. When she found me near her cottage a few months ago, I was half dead. A part of me wished I was. But, she mended my physical wounds the best she could and made me strong enough for our journey here. My mental wounds will take more time to heal—if they ever do.

After lunch, Rowan steals me away from the group so that we can have a little time together. War and Griffin decide to take their wolves out on a quick run while Lycus and Estelle head back inside.

Rowan is wearing a bralette and a maxi skirt made of flowy material. I reach out to touch her swollen belly, knowing she wouldn't mind. My sisters and I do not have many boundaries with each other.

"I can't believe you are pregnant," I say. "Are you all feeling okay today? I really don't know how I healed you."

"We are all doing great. War listens for their heartbeats all of the time. He says that they are all beating strong again."

That's good. That's really good. I have been worried that whatever magic I used would somehow reverse itself—as if it would realize that I shouldn't have been able to use it in the first place and the universe would take it all back. But it has been a few days and she is still okay. "I was so scared when I first saw you," I confess. Rowan pulls me into a tight hug as my eyes well up in tears. I can tell that she is crying too. Seeing her lifeless, pale body laying in a puddle of blood was one of the worst moments of my life. I was so afraid when I walked towards the giant, snarling black wolf and pleaded with him to let me help.

"I promise we are okay. Heka, that's War's grandmother, believes that my body would have healed itself after the baby was doing better, but I really appreciate the boost that you gave me. I know that it must have been awful for you guys to see."

I look down to my hands that haven't stopped shaking since I walked into the lodge and look closely at the shimmery moon tattoos that now decorate my skin. The only proof that I had any magic at all. "What does all of this mean?" I ask.

Rowan pulls me over to a comfy seating area further into the garden. "Do you want the long or the short?"

I smile. That is something that I often asked her while she was growing up.

"Let's start with the short." I'm not sure if I have the bandwidth for the long right now.

"Okay, well, I know that Griffin has mentioned that you are True Mates, right?"

I nod. Still not fully understanding or maybe accepting the weight of that. I know that True Mates are believed to share a soul. Soulmates is what we would have said back in my world—though I don't think that many people back on Earth actually believed in the shared soul thing. A love like that isn't something that I ever believed I would find.

"Some True Mates are additionally blessed by The Moon. Apparently, it is incredibly rare—so the fact that we are both marked is wild. Basically, the wolves believe that there is The Mother, who gives life, and her Mate, The Moon. The Mother decided all True Mate pairings at creation, but The Moon blessed a select few with additional magic, making them Moon Touched...sorry, that might not have fully been the short version. It is all a little complicated."

"Estelle told me that Mates can share each other's magic."

"Yes. In a few different ways. And since we came here as boring, non-magical humans, we can gain magic when we bond with our Mates. I thought that the Moon Touched magic appeared at that time as well—at least mine did—but you were able to tap into yours before the bond so I'm not sure what triggers that."

Remembering my conversation with Griffin earlier, I try to keep the conversation light. "And your moon magic granted you a magic pussy and the ability to help others get knocked up?"

Rowan snorts. "Bingo."

"And mine let me heal you, but I do not know how or why or if I can ever do it again." That has been bothering me. The unknown of what I did and if I can do it again.

"Do you feel any different from before you came into this world?"

I feel completely changed—but not because of any magic. "I don't think so. What does it feel like?"

"For me, it feels kind of like a cloud of something within my chest. When I use my magic, I imagine strings or tree roots to push my magic through. I focus on love and health—but it might be different for you. War told me that it feels different for him.”

“And what else did you get from War—other than the three nuggets you are growing.”

Rowan smiles, rubbing her hand over her belly. “Quicker healing. Most likely an extended lifespan. I can communicate mind to mind with War—though I haven’t been able to connect with anyone else. War thinks that I gained a more sensitive sense of hearing, though I just think that he snores obnoxiously loud.”

“And if I bond with Griffin, I would gain those things too?”

“Most likely. Though, Griffin has an extra sensitive sense of smell—not hearing. Oh, and you will probably be able to understand all languages like they can.”

“What do you mean?”

“Well, right now, we are both speaking in English, obviously. But, they can understand us even though English is not their language. They evolved over time to be able to understand all languages since there are so many spoken throughout this world. Now that I am bonded, I can understand their language. I don’t even realize that it is happening. It all sounds like English to me.”

“That doesn’t seem possible.”

"I know," she laughs. "But it is. A lot of things in this world are like that." She pauses for a moment, chewing on the inside of her cheek. "And it is when, not if," she spits out.

"What?"

"You said 'if I bond with Griffin.' It is not an if. It is a when. He is yours and you are his whether you do the ceremony or not. Bonding will just make you stronger and less fragile in this world where everyone is stronger than you."

So I don't have a choice? I let that sit for a bit. I'm not sure if I am upset that I have no choice or if I am relieved that it is one less thing that I need to make a decision about. I understand what she is saying—about needing to make myself stronger for this world. I wish I could have been stronger in our world. Predators existed in that world too—they just didn't burst out of their skin like they do here.

I just don't think that I am in any condition to enter into a relationship with someone. Griffin deserves better than the broken shell of someone he has no choice but to be with. Because that is true too, isn't it? I don't have a choice but to be his Mate—but he doesn't either. He is stuck with me. Saddled with my nightmares. My pain. My trauma.

How can I expect that of him?

This entire conversation is making me feel itchy, so I let Rowan know that I am tired and head back to my room for a bath.

Chapter Four

Griffin

It has been a while since I have gone for a run without any real reason behind it. Bade and War spend a lot of time out in the wilds of their territories, moving between outposts. I occasionally get called out to deal with something, but most of my time is spent at the lodge and within the main village. While Bade runs our military and War coordinates hunting, the Nighthowl pack mostly supports the packs with trade. We create textiles, pottery, and jewelry. We have the largest supply of books out of the three packs and keep record of our history.

My pack does not require much from me, which suits me just fine.

But it is nice to go for a run with my brother every now and then. I follow War as his large wolf, the same size as mine but with a pure black coat instead of my varied shades of brown, leads me through the forest just outside the village. It has been a while since I have been over here, but I believe he is taking us over to a group of hot springs that we would visit as kids.

Once I see them up ahead, I sprint, challenging War to a race. He might be a bit stronger than me, but I have always been faster. I leap into the water, shifting as I come back up for air. War does the same and we are both laughing.

"How are you doing with all of this," he asks me. 'This' being Ramsey.

"It has not been long, but my wolf really does not like that she has refused to sleep in my quarters," I share.

War nods, understanding the need to share the space with your Mate. "Things with Ro and I were different since we were out in the wilds. She did not have any other option but to share a space with me. But I slept on the floor and then in a chair until she was comfortable enough with me. Ramsey will get there. This is all a lot for someone to process."

It *is* a lot for someone to process. But I think that there is more to it than that for her. "I do not want to push her too hard, but I worry that if I give her too much space, she will never try to become comfortable. I doubt Rowan was as hesitant to open up to you as Ramsey is with me. Other than letting me stay in orbit around her, she has not given any indication that she feels the bond like I do."

"Is she doing okay otherwise? I know it has not been long since she met you, but she has been in our world for the same amount of time as Rowan. I would think that she would be acclimated to some of the ways of our world by now."

"She told me that Estelle shifted in front of her one time, but otherwise, she has remained in her human form. They avoided contact with anyone else while they traveled here—not knowing who they could trust."

I need to talk through some of my theories on what is causing her sometimes odd behaviors, but I do not want her to feel like I am sharing something private. Whatever she is going through—she is not an open book about it. I have a feeling that if I had not heard her nightmares or witness her panic at breakfast, she would not have told me anything. *That* is something that we will need to work on.

"She is guarded—afraid," I say. "But she is okay being around me. She is quiet but asks questions. She is open to sharing some things but then firmly tells me when she does not want to talk about something else. Maybe she is just processing.”

“Rowan told me that Ramsey is very pragmatic. She might just need more time.”

“I am sure that she does. Hopefully she will be a little more open with Rowan.” Quietly, I add, “I think that something happened to her before she came here.”

War nods again. “Ro told me that she had been drugged and locked in a cage. She had been beaten and truly may have died if Heka had not been able to rid her of infection. Maybe Estelle will know more.”

“Yeah, maybe.” I cannot help the wide range of thoughts filling my head as to what may have happened to her. I fear that it was something horrible, but I do not know how to bring it up with her. Or, if I even should. “I do not want her to feel like I am digging around for answers behind her back, though. You know how I am when there is an issue that I think I can solve.”

War snorts. “A dog without a bone.”

“What?”

“Oh nothing. It is just a phrase that Rowan used one time. I think that you should just give her time and space, but not too much. Gently push at her walls.”

“Yeah,” I say nodding, “Okay, I can do that. I really want her in my quarters though. So far, I spend each night laying outside her door. I feel a bit crazy, but I need to hear her breathing."

"You are not crazy. That is your wolf. You will feel unsettled until the bond is sealed."

It is incredibly warm today, so I hop out of the hot springs and race War to the lake that is a little further into the forest. Once we have cooled off, we make our way back to the lodge.

I am really hoping that Rowan was able to answer some of Ramsey's questions.

When I get back to the lodge, I head straight for the room next to the library—the room that Ramsey has slept in since she arrived—hoping to find my Mate. However, when I get there I notice that everything has been cleared out. She did not have a lot of personal items, but the wardrobe has been emptied, and the bathroom is without her toothbrush and soaps.

I begin to panic, thinking that she has left, but then I look within myself and follow the pull between my soul and hers.

The closer that I get, the bigger the smile on my face. I quietly enter my room to find Ramsey sound asleep in my bed. I check the wardrobe and the bathroom, which now have her items next to mine.

Without waking her, I move over to my plush chair by the fireplace and pick up the book that I started a few days ago.

I may not know everything that I need to know about Ramsey, but this is a step in the right direction. She moved into my space and is comfortable enough to sleep in my bed. I would never presume that this means I am welcome to join her, but I love that she is going to wake up in my space, smelling like me.

Most True Mate relationships move quickly, but we can do this in small steps.

I must have fallen asleep because some time later, I wake with a blanket draped over my lap. My bed is empty, but it sounds like Ramsey is in the bath. I quickly change into fresh clothes and wait for her to finish getting ready for dinner.

Ramsey startles when she walks out of the bathroom. She is pure perfection, skin pink and glistening from the bath water. Her dark hair is loose and slightly wavy. She is wrapped in only a towel, sending all of my blood to my cock.

She rushes over to the wardrobe to pull out the other dress that I borrowed from Rowan this morning.

I want to see everything that she is hiding under that towel, but I know that she would prefer some privacy.

I attempt to discreetly adjust myself before rising and clearing my throat. "I will give you some privacy," I say as I walk into the bathroom, shutting the door behind me. I splash some cool water on my face as I try to talk my dick down. I should probably apologize to War for making fun of him for having a constant hard on around Rowan. This Mate stuff is no joke. I debate taking my cock in my hand but then hear a small knock on the bathroom door.

I open it up and see Ramsey, dressed and looking uncertain.

"Is it okay that I'm here? I probably should have asked before moving myself into your space, but I felt brave for a moment after talking to my sister and now I am worried that I overstepped," she blurts out.

My face softens, "Of course, I want you here," I reassure her. I reach out to tuck a strand of her hair behind her ear, a move that I have successfully done before, but she flinches so I pull my hand back and offer a smile instead. "You are my Mate. This space is yours too."

Ramsey nods, wringing her hands, still nervous.

"I don't know if I am ready for this...any of this," she confesses. "Honestly, I do not know what I will ever be ready for. There are some things that, um, I am dealing with. I don't want to talk about them right now, but maybe with time I will be able to. I want to get to know you, if that is something that you are interested in."

I smile and hesitantly reach out to brush her cheek with my thumb. This time, she does not flinch away. "I want to get to know you too."

I want that more than anything.

"Do you think it would be okay to have dinner with your family and Rowan tonight? I'm not sure what you usually do, but I want to get comfortable with people and family seems like a good place to start. It won't happen if I don't try."

"Yes. We usually have dinner together every night. All our meals, actually. Plus, we are starting a family game night back up soon now that Rowan is here to keep War in line."

She snorts and then starts to laugh. I must make a face because she quickly calms herself down, biting on her lips to quiet herself. I brush my thumb against her mouth, wanting her laugh to continue. It is my favorite sound. She takes a sharp breath but does not shy away from my touch.

"I'm sorry, I don't mean to laugh." Her voice is slightly raspy. "The image of wolves playing games just popped into my head and reminded me of a famous painting back in my world of dogs playing a card game."

I offer her a big smile. "We do not usually play as wolves, though that could be fun." Reminding myself that I need to gently push at her walls, I add, "We do not have to start it back up tonight, if it is too much. It is just an option if you are feeling up to it."

"Thank you. Let's play it by ear."

I lead Ramsey out of the room and direct her towards the dining room. She tenses and her breathing becomes choppy when I place my hand on her lower back, so I pull my hand away. She releases a slow breath but does not say anything.

Interesting. She does not always flinch away when I touch her face or her hair but touching her back seems to bother her more. I make note of that, wanting to be aware of any boundaries that she sets with me.

Baby steps. I can do that.

Chapter Five

Ramsey

I didn't think this through, and now I am beginning to spiral. I moved into Griffin's room after my chat with Rowan, because I realized that it was going to happen anyway. I did not know that he had been sleeping in the hall until I stumbled upon him this morning. I thought that he would just stay in his room and I could stay in mine—far away from where anyone would hear my nightmares.

But he heard.

Every night, he was there, and he heard my nightmares. He woke me up and stayed close to me in case I needed him again. He told me that he had been awake, reading in the library. Maybe he was. But then he was asleep against my door in the morning, and I just knew that he would continue to sleep there for as long as I chose to stay in that room.

It is inevitable for another reason too. This entire thing with Griffin—being his Mate—I can feel it. I haven't admitted it out loud, only just recently having the courage to admit it to myself. But the pull that Ro described to me earlier has been something that I have felt since I woke up in this world. I thought that it was just me. I thought that it was just my human body feeling out of sorts in a new environment. I explained it all away without talking to anyone about it. But now I know. And it is even harder to ignore now that we have met each other.

So, I know that he is my Mate. My True Mate. Even without the matching marks on our hands, I could logically follow the clues and come to this decision. But what I am having trouble wrapping my head around, is how I can feel so strongly for someone who I just met. I *crave* him on a level that I have never felt before. Ro explained how quickly everything happened between her and War, but she has always been the most spontaneous out of the three of us. Feelings over facts. But I have never had feelings for a man before—not like this at least. Attraction, sure. But this is deeper. It is like I feel him in my bones and this craving that I feel for him overwhelms my senses. I *need* to be around him. Which is why I am in his space. The idea of him being uncomfortable so that I can be slightly more comfortable makes me feel uncomfortable. It is a vicious cycle that quite frankly seems asinine when I could simply move to his room and allow him the comfort of being in his own space.

All of that made sense when I thought it out logically. But now that I am faced with the very real reality that I am about to sleep in the same room as my gorgeous, kind, patient, soulmate, the panic is threatening to take hold.

I am just not ready. Like I told him, I don't know if I ever will be. What I experienced before I came here—what was done to me—has forever changed me. I am not the same Ramsey as I was before. And that is okay. I have accepted that. Well, I am working on accepting that. It is hard to pull myself out of the mess that haunts my dreams. And it is hard to trust someone enough to let them help me. With Estelle, I had no other option. She found me and healed me. She must have woken from my nightmares, but she only ever asked me about them once. She didn't push me. And that was what I needed at the time. It is what I still need, I think. But, maybe one day, I will be able to offer up an explanation.

At dinner, I tried. Everyone sat in the same order as we had for lunch. I mostly spoke to Ro, but I did force myself to ask Lycus a question. I was trying to make things less awkward after I ran out of the room at breakfast—so I did it. I even looked up, quickly making eye contact. He looks so similar to Griffin, though his hair is black like War's and his eyes are a vibrant green instead of the brilliant blue that his sons have. I think he answered my question, but I couldn't tell you what his response was. The sound of blood rushing through my ears drowned out his words. But I did it. I survived it. And I am proud of myself. If anyone other than Griffin noticed, they didn't say anything. He quietly took my hand in his and gave it a squeeze under the table. His touch helped bring me back.

Anytime I finished something on my plate, Griffin immediately replaced it with more. It was a simple thing, but I have always been the one to take care of everyone else. I didn't realize how nice it feels to have someone looking out for me. I have never had that before.

And now, I am sharing his space. I am pretending to get ready for bed, even though I know that I am not going to be able to sleep a wink. I brush my teeth, wash my face, and slip on one of Griffin's shirts. I step out of the bathroom, feeling a bit awkward, unsure as to what to do with my hands or what to say.

"Is underwear not a thing here," I blurt out as I awkwardly tug at the hem of the shirt I'm wearing.

Griffin throws his head back and barks a laugh. "I'm sorry. It is just that your sister asked the same thing. It really is not a thing here. Clothes are very optional for shifters. But we have all started wearing them more around the lodge."

"So, you all just hang out together naked? Isn't that dicey? What if you pop a boner when you are sitting next to your grandma?" My face instantly heats, and I cover my mouth with my hand. Why do I always vomit words when I am nervous?

Griffin's booming laughter in response makes me relax a little bit.

"I have never heard it called a 'boner' before," he says, wheezing. "Now that I think about it, that is probably why War has started wearing pants more often. I have always enjoyed clothes. I like the style aspect of them. But War and Bade hardly ever dressed before. Now that War has a constant boner, it would probably make meetings slightly inappropriate."

"He should probably get that checked out." I smirk. "Consult a doctor. I don't think that it is healthy to be hard that much."

"Probably, though that would be awkward since his doctor is his grandmother."

I snort, loving that our conversation is easy—though slightly inappropriate.

Feeling a little more at ease, I make my way over to the bed and crawl in. Griffin stays seated in his chair by the fireplace. The blanket that I put over him earlier is over his lap.

"I know that we didn't start up family game night tonight, but would you like to play a game with me?" Falling asleep is not going to come quickly to me—it never does anymore—so maybe I can use this time to get to know him better.

Griffin sets his book down and moves his chair closer to the bed. "Which game would you like to play?" he asks.

"I was thinking that we could each ask five questions. The answers can be as simple or detailed as we are comfortable sharing, but everything must be true."

"I would love to. Why don't you go first," he suggests.

"Okay. Um, what is your favorite book?"

"Ooh, that is a tricky one, but I do have an answer. My favorite books, plural, are my mother's journals. She wrote in them every day, detailing her life, which is interesting, but they are my favorite because I can still smell her scent on them. I like to read them when I am missing her."

"Rowan told me that you have a heightened sense of smell. I am not sure if I would like that, to be honest."

"It is a blessing and a curse," he chuckles.

"Your turn to ask," I say.

"Tell me something about you that not many know."

"Hmm. I have an eidetic memory. It came in handy when I was studying to become a nurse. Where my classmates struggled to memorize anatomy or even proper dosing, it was easier for me. The pictures and charts just stay locked in my head."

"Did you always want to be a nurse? Oh, sorry. It was your turn to ask a question."

"That's okay. I actually wanted to become a veterinarian, but I couldn't afford to be in school that long. I needed to be able to provide for my sisters. The program that I was in allowed me to work in the hospital and earn a wage while working on my degree. I worked at other jobs too," I explain. "I did learn to love it, though. I like helping people—taking care of them."

"If that is something that you want to do here, we are always in need of good healers."

"I would like that." Realizing that I have been staring at him, smiling, for longer than appropriate, I cleared my throat. "Do you, um, like being Alpha?"

"My brothers and I grew up knowing that we would share the role as Alpha. We decided early on that we would divide the pack, creating three packs that would focus on different aspects of pack life but then share those resources. We became Alphas at such a young age—we were only 17—so it was a struggle in the beginning. But I really do enjoy being the Alpha to the Nighthowl pack. I might not feel the same if I oversaw one of the other two, though. Military operations and hunting have never appealed to me the same way that art and knowledge do."

After only knowing him for a short time, I can already tell that Nighthowl is the best fit for him. I haven't met Bade but just comparing him to the snippets that I have learned about War, I can tell that Griffin is gentler, more polished. "I think that is part of why I am more comfortable with you," I confess. "I mean, you are obviously still huge, and you can turn into a giant wolf whenever you want, but you have never tried to intimidate

me—not with your size or your words. And I...I want you
to know how much I appreciate that."

Griffin reaches out to hold my hand. I let him. We
sit there for a minute before he lightens the mood. "What
is your favorite food?"

"Ice cream," I reply without any hesitation. "Do you
have that here?"

His brow crinkles as he thinks. "Not quite. But we
do have a sweet, thickened cream that we eat with
desserts. Rowan ate an entire pan of cobbler with cream
on top the other day. I was supposed to keep that secret
though, so you didn't hear it from me."

I giggle. "I think I am going to make it my goal to
make ice cream here. The base is probably similar to what
you are describing. We just need to make it super cold and
add in yummy things like small pieces of other desserts.
Cooking is actually something that I want to learn how to
do better. I know the basics, but I have never really had
the time to go beyond just keeping us fed."

"I'm sure we can make that happen," he says with
a smile.

We continue asking each other questions, not
caring whose turn it is or how many we have asked, until
late in the night. I feel my eyes growing heavy, but I am
nervous to sleep. I know that I am safe with Griffin, but

the nightmares are embarrassing. I don't want him to see me like that.

Eventually, I cannot keep my eyes open any longer. I feel Griffin pull the blanket up further around me, tucking me in. As I drift off to sleep, I hear him softly whisper a goodnight.

I am back in the cell. The hard floor bites into my bare knees and the single light bulb flickers above me. The smell of unwashed bodies, dirt, and blood makes my stomach turn. I hear footsteps approaching, so I move down to my side, pretending to be asleep. Maybe they will leave me alone if I am asleep. It has never worked before, but I know that if I make myself small, compliant, they will not be as harsh. They are here to give me another dose of whatever drug they are trying to control me with, but I never swallow it. I hide it under my tongue and then spit it into my waste bucket after they leave. They used to inject the medicine into my veins. I couldn't stop the high that it caused. Maybe I should give in and let the oblivion take me. At least then, I wouldn't remember what they do to the others. What they do to me. The high could turn the screams into something that they aren't. It could

help. But, if I give in, I will never claw myself back out. And I need to find a way out. I can't risk the temporary reprieve. I will become addicted to the feeling of not feeling. So, I spit out the pills and am forced to remember.

He walks in. I do not know which 'he' it is, it doesn't matter. They are all the same. 'Get up,' he demands, touching my body roughly. Pain shoots through me where he pushes on my battered skin. I have not had enough time to heal since the last visit someone paid to my cell. I block it out and slowly open my eyes—keeping them half lidded and drowsy. He squeezes my cheeks, forcing my mouth open and he shoves a pill inside. I quickly force it under my tongue. 'Now be a good whore while I give you something to wash that down with.' He unbuttons his pants and pries my mouth open wider.

There is screaming coming from another cell. He is distracted, smirking at whatever hell his buddy is inflicting on one of the other girls. He isn't distracted long—just for a moment—just long enough for me to spit out the pill before I am forced to swallow. He turns back to me, slapping me across the face for daring to shut my mouth. He steps closer, bringing the smell of sweat and cigarettes with him. I close my eyes and just wait for it to be over.

I wake up gasping. I can't get enough air. My lungs are screaming, and tears track down my face.

"You are okay," Griffin says softly. "You had a bad dream." He reaches out to hold my hand, but I flinch at the contact. He places his hand next to mine on the bed. "Is this okay?"

I look down at our hands. His is so much bigger than mine but I can't help but think how perfectly it would feel holding mine. I lean into the comfort of him just being next to me as I get my breathing under control. I wish I could allow more contact, but I am afraid of how easily I might be triggered right after my nightmare. Griffin seems to understand.

"Is there anything that I can get you?"

What I need is a bath, so that I can scrub it all away. I need to get clean. But I can't tell him that. He will think that I am crazy, and I will have to tell him why. I can't tell him. I should have stayed in my own room. He shouldn't have to deal with this—with all of my broken parts.

"Maybe just some water," I rasp.

Griffin immediately moves to get me some fresh water. After taking a few sips, I snuggle back down into bed.

"Do you feel better, Angel?"

I nod, even though tears continue to fall. I really wish I could accept the comfort that he so freely offers me. He reaches out again, to wipe my tears away. This time, I let him.

"Do you want to talk about it?" he asks quietly.

I shake my head as a sob breaks free.

"I really wish I could hug you right now, pretty girl," he confesses.

I want that too. I want to be able to handle that. I just know that I can't. I'm not ready. But maybe...

"Do you..."

"What is it, Angel?"

"Do you think that you could shift? I think that I really need that hug. I might be able to handle it if I pretend you are just a cuddly dog."

His face softens. "Of course." He stands up to head into the bathroom. Before he leaves the room, he turns back towards me. "Even if this does not work, I am proud of you for trying."

That makes me cry harder. He might not know why I am like this. He might not have any idea about the horrors that I relive every night. But he sees me. And so far, he is not running away.

He returns a moment later, leaping up onto the bed. I open up my arms and he lets me pull him into a hug, burying my face into his fur. I breathe in his amazing scent. Whether he is a wolf or a man, Griffin always smells like a chai latte. I would bottle it up if I could.

I snuggle down further, dragging him with me. I let his comfort wash over me and for the first time since the nightmares started, I am able to fall back to sleep without scrubbing myself clean.

Chapter Six

The next few days fly by as I try to get my bearings here at the lodge. I spend a lot of time during the day with Rowan and Heka, attending appointments and helping around the clinic. They filled me in on the fertility issues that the wolves are having. The amount of loss that they are facing is staggering, and I want to be able to help in any way that I can.

When I have quiet moments to myself, I try to access the magic that I used with Rowan, but I do not feel any of it. It is just gone.

Everyone thinks that it will come back. Either with time or by sealing the bond. Apparently magic has a sort of well and it is possible that I emptied mine when I healed Ro. It should replenish itself, but nobody really knows for sure. Other than Ro, there aren't any other living beings with Moon Touched magic that we can ask. Griffin does not feel anything different with his magic, other than his pull to me. And War only feels a difference through his connection with Ro. We are wading so deep into the unknown that everything is just trial and error. Mostly *me* trying and erroring as I struggle to keep my head above water.

But in the meantime, I know that I can use the skills that I learned by working in busy New York emergency rooms. I can focus on that. The medicine and medical supplies are a little different, but it doesn't take me long to get comfortable in the clinic.

Today, a mother named Eden is coming in for an appointment. From what I have learned, she is the woman who delivered Ro to Zuri, so right off the bat, I don't like her. Ro tells me that she is actually a really kind woman. She was Ro's first friend here—but I am not sure that I can ever forgive her for putting Ro and her babies in so much danger. Even if it was in an effort to save her own children who had been taken by Zuri earlier that day. There had to have been another solution.

War, apparently, agrees—which makes me like him a little more. Griffin has remained neutral, though I get the feeling that he would feel very strongly if it had been me that was put in that position.

Everyone is on edge as we await her arrival. Even Heka, who insisted on having Eden's appointment at the lodge instead of at their home, looks uneasy. Ro is adamant that she attends the appointment since Eden is one of the women who we know became pregnant with the help of her magic. War refuses to let Ro attend the appointment without him there to keep her safe. Honestly, the entire situation is a clusterfuck. But I will do my best to remain professional. I have treated prisoners, gang members, and abusers. I can treat her.

While I am feeling a little more comfortable, War does still make me nervous. He terrified me that first day that I met him—but I do understand that he was protecting Ro. Meeting anyone under those circumstances is not ideal. I stood my ground despite his massive wolf intimidating me. Hopefully I won't always be this nervous around him, but only time will tell. Luckily, for this appointment, he stays on the other side of the room, holding Ro tight to him while she rolls her eyes.

Trying to cut the tension in the air, I decide to introduce myself as Eden walks into the room. Right after

I reach out to shake her hand, the door swings open again and a man walks in, positioning himself next to Eden. Feeling like I cannot breathe, I step back, putting as much distance as I can between us by plastering myself to the wall. Everyone notices. I can feel their eyes on me as they stare. How could they not? I instantly shut down. My labored breaths fill the otherwise silent room and the space around me becomes hazy in my panicked eyes. Just as I am about to rush out of the room, the door opens again, and Griffin calmly walks into the room in his wolf form. He presses his body against my side, allowing me to lean against him and tangle my hands in his fur while I regain control over my breathing.

I am not sure who called for him, and there is really not enough room for his massive form in this already packed exam room—but I am beyond grateful.

Eden offers me a smile and then introduces herself and her Mate, Arlo. They are True Mates, but not Moon Touched. They have two kids and are expecting twins this time around.

It is awkward to have this appointment with me standing in a corner, unable to step closer to the expectant mother, but I try to make the most out of it. Heka does the physical aspects of the job—measuring Eden's belly and stuff like that, but I can still ask questions. "How have you been feeling? I am just learning about the differences in gestation between shifters and humans, but it seems like you are right on track. Do you feel the babies moving every day?"

"Oh, yes. I can feel them kicking around in there. I have more energy this pregnancy than I did with my others. Everything seems to be going okay, I think."

Heka pokes and prods at Eden's belly, nodding as she does. Then she lowers her ear to Eden's stomach.

"Two strong heartbeats," she says.

It is amazing to me that she is able to hear the babies with just her ears. Back in New York, we would use an ultrasound or a fetal doppler.

Working up the courage, I take a small step towards where Eden is stationed on the exam table. "Would you mind if I have a feel?" I ask.

Eden nods as I slowly approach her with wolf Griffin at my side. Arlo takes several steps back, allowing me to get closer to Eden without getting closer to him. I glance over at War and give him a small nod in thanks. He must have been the one to get Griffin here and ask Arlo to maintain the distance between us.

I gently put my hands on Eden's belly, pressing just hard enough to feel two little bodies moving and grooving. "They seem to be doing great," I say with a small smile.

We talk for a little longer about the symptoms she is experiencing, and Heka gives her an updated timeline for when she expects the babies to be due. Shifters have a shorter gestational range than humans, though it can vary a bit, so Heka likes to make a reasonable guess based on how everyone is developing at each appointment.

I remind Eden that she needs to notify us immediately if she experiences any extreme symptoms. Or, if she has any bleeding at all. Then, they leave, scooping their children up on their way out.

"Well, that went okay," Rowan says. "Do you feel silly for being a bit overprotective, Big Guy?" she asks War.

"Never. It is impossible for me to be overprotective of you. You deserve all of the protection, all of the time," he responds.

She rolls her eyes as she pushes him out the door. "Go do something important. Leave the doctoring to the pretty ones."

She laughs as War growls in response.

"Griffin, you can stay. You are much prettier." She makes her words loud enough that War would be able to hear her even if he did not have advanced hearing.

"You are going to pay for that sass with your ass," War yells back from out in the hall.

"That's some big talk, Big Guy. You know not to threaten me with a good time." I giggle at their banter and the fact that Ro is blushing. It is clear that she is absolutely smitten with her Mate. He is good for her.

The rest of the appointments that are coming in are just women, so I discreetly thank Griffin for his help and let him know that I will be okay to finish out the afternoon with just Heka and Ro. I'm sure that he has other stuff that he could be doing.

I leave the clinic a few hours later and head towards Griffin's quarters. He arranged for a clothier to come in so I can have some clothes made. I am exhausted from my earlier panic attack and all of the appointments that followed, but I have been wearing the same two borrowed dresses, in addition to Griffin's shirts, and I would love to have a couple more options.

It isn't until I am walking into Griffin's room that I face yet another issue. The clothier is a man. I freeze in my spot, unable to leave the doorway. My breathing becomes strained, and I start to see black spots in my vision.

Panic attack.

Again.

And I'm not talking about the little panic preview that occurred in the exam room this morning. This is a full blown, can't hear—see—think—do, attack. I am sweating. I am shivering. The world around me spins as my vision tunnels.

The clothier, who I am sure is a nice man, does not know what to do. Unfortunately, that makes two of us. My heart is pounding so fiercely, he must hear it. He steps forward, probably introducing himself, but all that I can see is a 'he' stepping closer. A 'he' moving so close, it would be easy for him to reach out and grab me. Touch me. The fear uproots my feet that have been bolted to the floor since the moment I saw him. I flee. I don't know where I am going—I just need to leave.

I find an empty room in a random hall. I'm not even sure whose part of the house I am in anymore. I close the door behind me and sink down into the corner, bringing my knees to my chest.

I'm not sure how long I sat there. It could have been minutes or years, but eventually, Griffin finds me. He approaches slowly, probably worried that I will freak out again. Mostly I feel embarrassed. That man did not do anything wrong, but I couldn't even walk into the room that he was in. I wish I wasn't so broken.

"You are not broken," Griffin says calmly. I must have said that last part out loud.

Griffin crouches down so that he is at my level. I can tell that he wants to hold me, but he gives me space. I don't think that I want space, but I don't know how to tell him that. What if he hugs me and I can't handle it? But what if he hugs me and it is exactly what I need?

I feel like I am made up of a million broken little pieces that have been cobbled back together. I might look the same on the outside, but I am not nearly as strong as I once was. One wrong move and I will break.

If I trust Griffin with this, will he help me put my pieces back together again?

It is exhausting doing it on my own.

"I should apologize to that poor man," I say quietly.

"Don't worry about it, Angel. I spoke with him. It is all okay."

I pull at my hair, needing something but I'm not sure what.

"But he didn't do anything wrong," I sigh. "I think that he might have even tried to help me, but I couldn't hear anything that he was saying over the sound of my body freaking out. I couldn't even walk into the room, Griffin. And you were so nice to set up that appointment for me." I know that I am rambling and crying and he is getting a front row seat to the mess that is my brain. I want to make it stop, but I can't.

"Can I sit next to you?" he asks quietly. I nod and he scooches closer so that our sides are touching. He gently untangles my hands from my hair.

"I'm not ready to talk about it yet," I admit as tears coat my cheeks.

"That's okay."

I slowly tip my head so that it is resting on his shoulder. We stay like that for a while. Not talking, just breathing and existing together.

Once my tears have dried, I look around the room that we are in. There are piles of random things. Most of it looks like junk but some of the items look like they could be different devices or tools.

"What is this place, anyway?"

Griffin looks around and huffs a laugh. "My dad likes to tinker. He thinks that he is an inventor—and I guess he is—but I do not think he has made anything actually work. When you have been alive for 500 years or so, I suppose you need to find hobbies to fill your time."

"500?!"

He nods.

"Wait, how old are you?" I ask.

"107," he says with a smile. "How old are you?"

"25. I knew that you had longer lifespans, but I didn't think about it before now."

"When we bond, you will have a longer lifespan too."

"I have some questions about bonding, but I don't think that I am quite ready to hear the answers."

"There is no rush," he says. "I will answer any questions you have when you are ready."

"When is the next full moon? That is when bondings happen, right?"

"In just over two weeks."

I nod. Letting that sink in. "And that is when you would like to bond?"

"Yes. But we will wait if you are not ready. I would wait a lifetime if that was what you need."

I snuggle closer to him, so my face touches his neck. He hesitantly puts his arm around me, rubbing my shoulder when I don't flinch away.

"Thank you, Griffin."

"For what?"

"Everything."

Chapter Seven

I arranged for Estelle to take Ramsey's measurements to give to the clothier. I am upset with myself for not making that accommodation from the start. I do not know why, but I do know that Ramsey has trouble being around males. I should have realized that having the clothier here could be an issue.

I was planning to be in the appointment with her, but I got caught up in the book that I was reading and lost track of time. I will not make that mistake again. I need to do better for her.

Ramsey has woken up every night from a bad dream. She usually wakes herself, but sometimes I pull her out of it. I quietly get her fresh water and then shift so that she can fall back to sleep while holding my wolf.

I sometimes ask her if she wants to talk about it, but she always shakes her head. Once she thinks that I am asleep, she sneaks out of bed to take a quick bath, crawling back into bed after she is done.

I do not know why she does this, but maybe the bath helps to soothe her in a way that I cannot. I am just happy that she comes back to me and am hopeful that she will be able to open up to me soon.

I am working in the library, when Rowan tracks me down.

"I thought I might find you here," she says.

"Is everything okay? Is it Ramsey?" I ask. Even when I am giving her some space, she is always on my mind.

"Oh, no. Ramsey is fine. She is in the clinic with Heka learning about medicinal herbs. I just wanted to see how you are doing."

"I am doing okay," I sigh. "I am trying my best to not overwhelm her. I do not think she is totally on board with the whole Mate thing yet."

Rowan squeezes my hand. "She will come around."

I do not know how to ask Ro if she has noticed anything different about Ramsey's behavior, or if she has confided in her. Other than mealtimes, I am not usually around when they are together.

"Has she said anything to you?" I sound vulnerable asking, but I just need to know.

"Honestly? Not much. But I'm sure she is just processing. Ramsey likes to have all of her facts sorted before making a decision."

I hesitate but decided to be more direct. "Has she said anything about her time before she came here?"

Rowan must not have been expecting that question because she looks shocked. Maybe she hasn't noticed any changes with her.

"No. She hasn't. Do you think that something happened? Oh god. I just assumed that she went to bed that night and then woke up here. Why would I assume that? Anything could have happened to her! I was drugged and kidnapped..." She gasps, "the men thing! I thought that it was just because you are all giants with wolves and muscles."

"I really should not have said anything. I am just worried about her."

"Did she say anything to you?" she asks.

"No. She told me that she will tell me when she is ready. Please don't say anything to her. I do not want her thinking that we are talking about her."

She worries her bottom lip for a minute but then promises that she will not say anything. We agree that we will both keep an eye on Ramsey though. She knows about Ramsey's hesitance around men, but I don't tell her about the nightmares. It seems too private to share—even with her sister. If Ramsey wanted Rowan to know, she would tell her, right?

The next day, I am called out to one of the outposts. Usually my Beta, Dex, can handle any issues that arise outside of the village, but one of the pack members is accusing another of stealing—which requires a trial by Alpha.

Ramsey is still sleeping when I need to leave, so I write her a note letting her know that I will be gone all day and might not be back until tomorrow. I hate leaving her, but I cannot risk bringing her with me. It is still too dangerous for her outside of the village, and I know that she will be safe in the lodge.

The issue at the outpost ended up taking more time than I would have liked, but I ran hard and made it back home in the early hours of the morning. I expect to find

Ramsey asleep in bed, given the time, but she isn't there. I listen closely, hearing her in the bath.

I curse at myself. She must have had a bad dream, and I was not here to calm her. I wait several minutes, her baths are always quick but get worried when she does not come back out. Slowly, I creep towards the bathroom and open the door a crack to peek inside to make sure she is okay.

What I find is far from okay.

Ramsey is in the bath. The water is so hot, steam fills the air, and her skin is bright pink. Her body is a patchwork of wounds. She has scrubbed her skin raw in several places, bleeding, and she is still going. The scalding water around her is tinged red. She has tears streaming down her face, but she is not making any sound. Her focus is detached—lost in thought.

It is as if she is not really here at all.

I do not think there is any way that I can approach her without startling her, so I walk directly to her and hope that I do not cause her more distress. She does not notice me until I climb into the bath with her, pulling the abrasive cloth from her hand. She is using one that is meant for cleaning the stone floors, not her delicate skin.

When her eyes connect with mine, I see fear, anger, and desperate sadness looking back at me. I pull her into my arms, holding her close to my chest. I do not know where to touch her, she has so many sore spots decorating her skin.

I gently run my hand down her back, trying to soothe her, and that is when I feel it. I keep my hand frozen in place on her back as my brain catches up to what my hand is feeling. Surely, I am wrong—but I need to find out. I pick Ramsey up out of the water and turn her in my arms so that I can see her entire back.

A low growl rips itself from my control. There is a brand on her lower back—burned into her skin, the edges raised and angry. A fucking brand. The design in the center is a monogram of some kind. Marking her as property. My fingers dust over the letters as I force myself back into a controlled calm. What horrors has my beautiful Mate survived?

She crumples forward and begins to sob.

"Shh… it's okay, Angel." I turn her around and cradle her in my arms, lifting us both out of the too hot water. I gently wrap a fluffy towel around, cursing as I notice the soft washcloths tossed to the side. She had to dig through them to find the roughest one. Tucking her into bed, I quickly dry myself off and then crawl into bed with her, holding her close.

A fucking brand.

"I need you to tell me what happened, Ramsey. I am so sorry if you are not ready to talk about it, but I need you to anyway." My voice shakes as I force myself to stay calm. "Please tell me."

I can feel her nod against my chest. She scoots up a bit, nestling her face into my neck, and takes a few deep breaths.

Then, she speaks.

"Rowan, Reese, and I went out to a club to celebrate Rowan's birthday. It was her 21st birthday—which meant she could legally drink alcohol—so she wanted to go out to have a few drinks and dance. I had been very casually seeing one of the bartenders at the club, so he was able to get us in and give us a booth for the night. We were having a great time dancing, but we got separated from each other. I am not sure where Rowan or Reese ended up at this point, but I went over to the bartender to ask him if he had seen them. That is when I felt a sharp pinch in my neck. A syringe. Someone had drugged me. I do not know how long I was out, but when I woke up, I was in a cell.

"A prison?"

"It felt like one," she continues. "I don't know how many cells there were or what most of the building looked like. I think it was in a warehouse or something, but I was usually blindfolded when I left my cell for any reason. I could hear others in their cells but could only see the inside of mine. At first, there were other girls with me. But they were taken. They didn't come back."

She chokes out a sob and tries to take deep breaths to continue on.

"Take your time, Angel."

"They only used the injection in the beginning. Then, they switched to pills. I knew that if I let them drug me, there was no way that I would find a way out, so I pretended to take them and then spit them out after they left. I would act sluggish and unfocused when they were there so that they didn't realize what I was doing."

I kiss her forehead. "You are so brave, love."

She chokes out a pained sob as she continues. "They would, um, touch me. Force me. Make me... They hurt me in ways that I can't...It's too hard to talk about."

I cannot stop my body from shaking, but I do my best to not squeeze her any tighter.

"I fought back at first, but they were always stronger. Fighting them made it worse. So, I just blocked it all out. My brain just went blank and I...I just got through it. They are the ones who branded me."

"That's what your nightmares are about?"

She nods. "Every night I end up back in that cell, reliving everything that was done to me. It is why I am afraid of men—why I have trouble being touched. My brain gets confused when I am approached. I get flashbacks of the fear that I felt before. The fear that I couldn't let anyone see because I was supposed to be drugged out of my mind."

I knew that something bad had happened. I even suspected that she was threatened or abused in some way by a man. But this? This is more horrific than I thought. She believes that she is broken, but all I see is strength.

"I am so sorry, Angel. Nobody should ever be forced into a situation like that. I promise that you are safe with me. I will protect you."

"I know you will," she says. "It is different with you. Even when I flinch sometimes, it is not because it is you. I want you to touch me. I think that I actually need you to. Please keep trying."

"I will, I promise." I place another soft kiss on her head. "I need you to tell me about the baths now. I noticed that you often take a bath after a nightmare, but I thought it was just a way to relax, reset, so that you could go back to sleep. But it is more than that, isn't it?"

She is quiet for a long time before she speaks. "In my nightmares, I am back in that cell. The smells, the grime, it all feels real. I can feel it coating my skin. Sometimes I can see it, even though it isn't there. The things that were done to me—I just feel so dirty. Like their hands left smudges on my soul. Having you with me has helped. I feel safe. But I still need to feel clean before I can really move on from it."

I carefully scan her body, remembering the places where she scrubbed the most. The tears that I have been trying to hold back pour from my eyes. Her arms, her neck, her chest, her inner thighs. I take a deep breath but do not make any effort to dry my face.

"And tonight, I was not here, so you had to scrub more?"

Ramsey nods. "It was a bad one. They are all bad, but some memories are worse. I don't even really feel it when this happens," she points to some of her raw spots. "It is like I get lost in the moment and am not aware of when I need to stop."

"I will make sure that I am always with you at night," I promise. "And I can help you bathe if you are comfortable with it. I do not want you to hurt yourself."

"We can try that," she agrees. I pull her even closer, wrapping my arm around her.

"Is this okay?" If she needed me to shift, I would. But after everything that she just shared with me, I need to feel her in my arms.

Ramsey nods, her eyes fluttering closed.

"Go to sleep, Angel. I will be right here."

Chapter Eight

Ramsey

Seven days since Griffin found me in the tub. Seven days of the same routine. We wake up each morning, get cleaned up and dress side by side. I work in the clinic; Griffin works in the library or has meetings with his pack members in the village. We eat all of our meals together—usually with the family—and then retire to our room after dessert or game night.

Every night, I wake up screaming from a nightmare. Every night, Griffin takes me to the bath and gently cleans my skin. Every night, he holds me to his body until I fall back asleep.

I haven't asked him to shift into his wolf since that night he pulled me out of the bathtub. The feel of his warm skin against mine is more soothing than anything else we have tried. I can see, and feel, his body's reaction to me, but he never asks for more.

Before we fall asleep for the night, we ask each other questions. Sometimes, they are heavy and important. Sometimes, they are light and goofy. They all make me feel closer to him. They all remind me that I am still a complete human being with likes and dislikes, opinions on major and minor things. I am still me—even if this new version of me is still a little tarnished.

Every moment spent with Griffin brings me back to life.

The full moon is only a week away and I need to ask the questions that I have been avoiding so far. But first...

"Is there a way for me to shave my legs? I noticed that Rowan's legs are always smooth..."

Griffin gives me a smile. "War shaves Rowan's legs for her with a sharp knife. It was one of the ways that he was able to make her more comfortable when she first came here."

"Oh..."

"Is that something that would make you feel more comfortable? Rowan explained that it is normal in your

world for women to remove some of their body hair—
though some keep their body hair like the females in this
world do.”

“Um. I think that it might help.” Now that Griffin
knows about my past, I have become better about
discussing my insecurities with him. “I don’t feel the
same, in my body, as I used to,” I confess quietly.

Griffin holds my hand in his. Over the last week, I
have become comfortable with him being close. I no longer
flinch when he touches me—unless he accidentally
touches my lower back when the brand marks me.

“I can help you with that, if you are comfortable
with it,” he offers.

I nod and then crawl out of bed, walking towards
the bathroom.

“Now?” he says with a chuckle.

“Why not?” I say with a shrug. “We can ask our
questions at the same time. It might help distract me a
bit.”

Griffin follows me into the bathroom. I run some
water into the tub while Griffin grabs a knife and some
scented oils. I keep my shirt on—well, his shirt—and sit
on the edge of the tub.

Several pieces of clothing have arrived for me over
this last week. Most of them are flowy dresses, but Griffin

also had some pajamas made for me. They are very comfortable, but I still choose to wear his shirts to bed most nights. There is a part of me deep down that likes being wrapped up in his scent.

"Can we talk about the bonding ceremony?" I ask.

He lathers my legs in the oil and then looks up at me. "Of course. What questions do you have?"

"I guess, well, Ro told me a little bit about her bonding ceremony. She said that she had to walk naked through the pack on her way to War."

"That is the traditional way—but we could have a more private ceremony. Maybe in the garden with only our family present?"

"I don't think that I could be naked," I say quietly.

He hesitates. "Because of the brand?" he asks.

I nod, blinking back the tears that are starting to well in my eyes.

"We can figure something else out. Traditionally, we would be naked so that there is nothing separating us from The Mother and The Moon. Jewelry is often worn though. Maybe a piece could be made that would cover the mark?"

"Could that be done in time?"

"Nighthowl is responsible for making all of the jewelry and textiles for the packs. We could have something made by tomorrow if we needed to."

"Are you sure that you want to bond with me, even knowing everything that you do." I hate the vulnerability in my voice, but I need to hear him say it.

Griffin sets the knife down that he was gliding over my bare legs, leaving only smooth skin behind, and brings his hands up to hold my face.

"I would bond with you right now if it was possible. I choose you in this lifetime and the next. My soul calls out to you and yours answers. I will stand by your side through every joy and every sorrow. The weight that you carry is mine to hold."

His words wrap me up in warmth. I know that he is content with what we have started to build together. But eventually, he will want more. We both will. "What if I am not able to ever give myself to you in the way that you deserve—the way that I want to?"

"You give me your mind freely. Your soul is already a part of me. Everything else will come with time."

"But what if..."

"But, if that is something that we never share, I will still be happily yours."

Feeling brave, I wrap my hand behind his neck and pull his lips to mine. I can hear the catch in his breath, not expecting this from me.

The kiss is hesitant at first. I run my tongue against the seam in his lips, which he opens for me. I deepen the kiss but keep it slow—searching. He meets my tongue stroke for stroke, giving me back what I am offering without asking for more.

It is perfect.

I pull away, breaking the kiss to catch my breath. He tips his forehead to mine, breathing me in.

After a long moment, I give him a small smirk and turn my face away. My cheeks are pink, and I am still slightly out of breath.

Griffin finishes up shaving my legs and pulls away to clean up. I hesitantly lift off my shirt and ask him to shave under my arms too. When he is done, he places a gentle kiss on my collar bone before turning away.

I have never shared something so intimate with another person before.

That night, I did not wake from a nightmare. I awoke tangled in Griffin's arms, the morning sun shining through the large window, and felt at peace.

Chapter Nine

For the entire day that follows, I go through the motions of my routine, but I cannot stop thinking about that kiss and how right it felt. I did not panic like I thought I would. I know deep in my soul that Griffin would never hurt me or force me. That one kiss was perfect—and it makes me want to try more with him. He woke up something in me that is fueled by my craving for him.

It is *those* thoughts that I have while sitting down for dinner with the family.

We received some amazing news earlier today. Bade has Reese. She is in this world. He will keep her safe. And I can allow myself to relax just a little more.

They are not able to travel back right away but will return when they can safely do so.

Rowan and I are obviously thrilled. Knowing that she is here and alive, makes everything that I went through to get here worth it. Ro is hoping that Reese will be here before she has the babies—though none of us really know when that will be.

Everyone is talking over each other—not in a rude way—but just in a comfortable, family way. It is something that we saw in movies but never really experienced growing up. It is crazy to me how quickly these people have become my family. I am feeling more and more comfortable with them, which is the only reason I can think of for what comes out of my mouth.

"Do shifters have normal sex or is it different?" I blurt, immediately covering my face with my hands.

War spits out his drink. Rowan cackles. Griffin's cheeks turn a lovely shade of red. Heka and Estelle smile. And Lycus, well, he just continues eating as if I didn't just ask the most embarrassing question at the dinner table.

"The mechanics are basically the same," Griffin answers quietly.

"Sure," Ro adds, "but, Rams, it is unlike anything I have experienced before." She then holds her hands out in front of her about a foot apart and waggles her eyebrows at me.

"Oh god," I whimper. I can't believe I started this conversation.

"Maybe this is a conversation you can have with your sister privately?" Griffin suggests.

I nod and bury my face in his shoulder.

We quickly get through dessert in an awkward silence and then I pull Rowan out of the room with me. She almost trips as she tries to keep up, causing War to growl and Rowan to giggle.

"Where are you taking me?" she asks.

I stop and look around. I really don't know where we should go to have this conversation.

"Maybe you should be leading," I tell her. She nods and then directs me through War's quarters and up into a secret room.

"I call this 'The Hideaway'. Their mother used this room to escape the crazy when she was alive. War told me that there are other secret rooms in the lodge. I wonder if Griff has one."

The Hideaway is cozy, reminding me of the small apartment that we lived in back in New York. Ro clearly spends a good amount of time here. There are blankets tossed casually on the couch and cushioned chairs. Plants weave between shelves and books—the entire ceiling is glass, lighting the space with the sun during the day and the moon at night.

"So…"

"What do you want to know? You know I will tell you anything. If it wasn't for your obvious embarrassment at dinner, I would have answered your questions then and there," she says.

I still have not told her about what happened to me, so I quickly dive in. I share everything that I told Griffin, including how he found me in the tub the other night, and everything leading up to our kiss last night. By the end, we are both crying and holding each other.

"I wish you would have told me sooner," she says.

"I know. I wasn't ready to tell anyone. Estelle must have known at least some of it but she never asked. I know that Griffin had his suspicions—how could he not when he has helped me through nightmares and panic attacks. But saying it out loud makes it real, and I needed to be strong enough first."

"I understand. I am just so sorry that it happened to you. I was drugged and taken too—but I was able to run away before anything really bad happened. They must have taken us to different places."

I nod. Griffin had already told me what he knew of Rowan's story. She had been beaten but not sexually assaulted. I was so relieved to know that she got away before anything like that happened. It makes me worry about Reese, though. If we were both taken, what are the chances that she wasn't?

"Now," Ro says while wiping our tears away, "what questions do you have about shifter sex?"

"The mechanics are the same?"

"Yes. Though they do have knots."

"Like in the omegaverse books Reese likes to read?"

"Yep. Just like that. It swells at the base and then locks you together until the swelling goes down."

I gulp. "And that feels okay? It doesn't hurt? How does it fit?"

Ro laughs. "It feels amazing, it doesn't hurt, and you just kind of make it fit. Our bodies can adjust to push a baby, or three, out. We can adjust to fit a massive cock and knot too."

"I can't believe that this is my life right now," I say, shaking my head. "I have seen Griffin's body. I really don't know how it will fit."

"If he's anything like War, which I am pretty sure he probably is, it will get even bigger. But I'm telling you, it is the best sex I have ever had—not that I had an amazingly adventurous sex life before coming here. But nothing else even comes close. I don't like to think about it because I am a bit of a possessive bitch, but these guys have been around for 100 years. They know what they are doing. They have the experience to back it up. War knows what I need without me even saying it. And he is down to try anything."

"Anything?" I gulp again. There are a lot of things that I have always wanted to try but haven't felt comfortable bringing up with a partner.

Ro takes my hands in hers and puts on her serious face. "The first night that War and I were intimate, he ate my ass and made me come so hard I almost blacked out."

"Oh my god!" I laugh, pushing her away playfully. "I have never done anything like that before. Honestly, I have never come from oral before at all."

She is laughing too. "I guarantee that is about to change."

"If I can be brave enough to try," I admit. "I am so worried that I will get triggered and freak out."

Ro wraps her arms around me and holds me tight. "You are safe with Griff. And, not just because he would never hurt you. If you do get triggered, he will stop and help you through it. It will be okay, Rams."

"Griffin said that we can make some modifications to the bonding ceremony. He explained the reason behind the nudity—but said he could have some sort of jewelry piece made to cover my brand. He is always so gentle and thoughtful of my needs."

"Can I see it?" she asks quietly.

I take a deep breath and then lift my dress up, showing her the mark on the small of my back. I can hear her gasp, but I don't turn around to see her face. I remember the shape of the heated iron but have not had the strength to look at the mark on my skin. I am thankful that it is in a place where I am not forced to see it every day.

"Once you are bonded, Heka can probably remove that for you. If that is something that you want. You would have faster healing and we could use Griffin's magical juju spit to heal it even faster."

"Magical juju spit?" I choke out as I spin back around to face my sister.

"He hasn't told you about that? Wolf spit can heal. It doesn't work for big things, but small cuts and scrapes are healed really quickly."

I think back to the night that Griffin found me in the tub, covered in sores from where I scrubbed layers of my skin away. I didn't even think about them the next morning—probably because they were mostly faded. He must have healed me when I was asleep. It probably should make me panic, to have his tongue on me without me knowing, but it doesn't. It wouldn't have been sexual for him. It was just another way for him to take care of me.

"And the bonding—it involves sex?"

"Yes. It creates a bit of an orgy if the pack is present. But for you and Griffin, it would be private. For wolves, bonding triggers a heat. Mine lasted longer than they typically do—but that might have to do with my magic pussy powers. Or maybe it was because it was my first heat and my body was going through a pretty wild change. We don't really know. But it is days of boning. You are still aware and in control of your actions, but you will be the horniest you have ever been in your life."

Would I be okay with doing that? If I know that it is Griffin and I know that we are both still in control of our bodies—I think that I might. With him, I feel like I might be brave enough for anything.

What I do know for sure is that I need to see if I can be intimate with Griffin *before* we bond. It would not be fair to put us through a heat filled with panic attacks.

"Oh, and if you do not want a whole batch of buns in your oven, Heka has some tea that you can both drink to prevent pregnancy. With me around, I highly suggest taking it if you are at all doubting."

Kids. I have always wanted to be a mother—but maybe not right now. I make a mental note to get that tea asap.

Ro and I chat for another hour or so before she starts to yawn. She walks me back to Griffin's—my—our room.

"Did you have a good talk with Rowan?" Griffin is in the process of changing when I walk in. He pauses when he sees me.

"Yes. I am sorry if I embarrassed you at dinner. I didn't mean to blurt it out like that. I just had a lot on my mind and my inside thoughts became words that were just spilling out of my mouth. I swear it was like I was watching it all unfold right in front of me, but I couldn't stop it from happening."

Griffin chuckles. "You didn't embarrass me. I was just a bit surprised, that's all."

"I can't stop thinking about our kiss," I confess.

Griffing walks slowly to me, reaching out and moving me closer. "Yeah? Me either."

"It was the best kiss that I have ever had," I say breathlessly. "I think that we should do it again. For science."

"Sure, for science," he holds my face in his hands. "To make sure that it was really the best?"

"Mmhmm."

Without any hesitation, Griffin crashes his mouth to mine, taking me in a hungry kiss. This kiss is not the gentle searching kiss that we shared last night. It is full of need. His tongue lashes into my mouth, catching my moans and stirring something within me that I wasn't sure I would ever feel again. Lust. Desire. Need.

I match his desire, pulling his lip into my mouth and biting down, causing him to whimper. The sound goes straight to my clit. I reach down to undo the ties on his pants. I know that he needs me to initiate it.

He lowers his lips to my neck, sucking on my pulse point.

"I don't know how much I am ready for. But I want to try."

"If you tell me to stop, I will stop immediately. Do you trust me, Angel?"

I nod. "I trust you." I really, really do.

"Let me take care of you," he says. Griffin backs me up to the bed, dragging my dress up over my head before gently laying me down.

"I want to see you," I say. I need him to be just as exposed as I am.

Griffin removes his pants before climbing up onto the bed with me. He sits on his heels, between my legs, with his massive cock jutting straight out from his body. I reach for him, sealing his mouth to mine as he settles over top of me.

"Is this okay?" he asks.

I nod my head.

"I need your words, pretty girl."

"Yes. This is okay. This is great, actually."

"Can I taste you?" His question causes a gush of arousal to run between my legs. His nose twitches and a low growl of pure need comes from his chest.

"You can. But I've never…I've never been able to come like that before."

"You will tonight," he says confidently.

Griffin moves his lips all over my body, kissing, sucking, biting as he works his way down. He pulls my nipples into his mouth, flicking them with his tongue before leaving gentle kisses on each breast.

By the time he reaches my pussy, I am dripping with desire and aching for his touch. After teasing me with nibbles to my thighs, Griffin licks me with one firm, steady sweep. He groans at the taste of me, reaching down to give his cock a hard pull to relieve some pressure.

"You taste so fucking good, Angel." I twine my fingers in his hair, holding his face where I need him.

Griffin laps at my center, plunging his tongue into my channel and flicking my clit. He pulls away, bringing his mouth to mine.

"Taste yourself. See how perfect you are," he says against my lips. I open my mouth and suck on his tongue, making us both moan.

"Good girl," he says as he returns his attention to my needy pussy.

Griffin alternates between fucking me with his tongue and teasing my clit. He holds my thighs wide open, his fingers pressing into my skin just enough that I might bruise. It isn't long before heat stirs low in my belly, building up to a blinding pressure that crashes through me. My vision goes splotchy, and I am yelling his name with my orgasm. I have never done that before either. I have always kept myself quiet. But with him, I couldn't hold myself back. Griffin helps me through it, swallowing down my release as if he cannot get enough.

Panting, I lay star-fished on the bed, trying to catch my breath.

My eyes are shut, but I can feel Griffin lay down beside me before he settles me close to his body. I blindly reach down to take him in my hand, but he grabs my hand and holds it in his.

"But that has to be bothering you," I say, gesturing to his erection. "It is only fair that I help you."

"Sex is not a transaction. Tonight was about you," he says. "This was a big step, Angel. I am so proud of you."

He leans into me, taking my mouth in another searing kiss.

"So, what would you rate that kiss? You know, for science." He gives me a panty melting smile.

I throw my head back and laugh. "Definitely a 10 out of 10."

Chapter Ten

Griffin

Waking up wrapped in Ramsey has become one of my favorite things. Her delicious honeysuckle and vanilla scent is the first thing that I notice. I breathe it in and feel settled in my soul. Her skin is impossibly soft. Her hard nipples press into my chest as she sprawls out half on top of me.

The full moon is tomorrow night, and we have decided that we are going to seal our bond. We still have not had sex—though we both enjoy having her fall apart on my tongue every night, and sometimes morning. Like this one.

Ramsey is awake, but still sleepy as I roll her to her back and move down between her legs. If she is going to take my cock tomorrow, I need to start stretching her out a bit. Teasing her clit with my tongue, I pump my finger into her. She is already so wet—she wakes up soaked for me. After a few minutes, I add another finger, slowly stretching her. She is so tight, it is going to feel amazing around my cock. I moan at just the thought.

After she shatters on my fingers, I bring them to her mouth so that she can have a taste. She moans around my fingers before I take her mouth with mine.

"Griffin," she whispers against my lips, "I want you to fuck me."

I pull away, wanting to look into her eyes. "Right now?" I ask.

Ramsey nods her head, grabbing my cock and positioning it at her entrance.

"I need to feel you. I need to know that I can share this with you before tomorrow night."

Understanding, I know that I need to give this to her. Not that it is any hardship. I want to live inside her sweet cunt for the rest of my life. But she is worried that she might be triggered and have a panic attack. I can show her that she is safe with me. I can show her that even if she does have an attack, she is safe in my arms.

No matter what. "I will go slow," I tell her. "If anything feels off, let me know and I will stop, okay?"

"I know. I am ready."

I press my mouth to hers again, needing her to feel the care that I have for her. Holding myself back from slamming into her, I gently push my cock forward. Her pussy greedily sucks me in. I know that she can take me, we were literally made for each other, but she is so tight that I begin to question how I am going to fit. When I get about halfway, I pause to look at her. She is flushed and panting, but not in any pain or panic.

"I feel so full," she moans.

"You are doing so well, Angel. Taking my big cock into your pretty pink pussy like a good girl."

Her walls flutter around at my praise. Ramsey loves being called a good girl and I plan on making sure that she always feels like one.

I push in even further, stopping every couple of inches so that she can adjust. Once I am fully seated, other than my knot, we both let out a breath. Sweat trickles down my neck from holding myself back.

"Is this okay?" I ask.

"Yes. I am ready for you to move."

I pull out almost all of the way before thrusting back in, making us both cry out. I hope that she does not judge me too harshly, but this is not going to be a long romp. She feels too fucking good. I continue thrusting in and out, hitting that spot inside her that I know brings her pleasure.

Her hands grip my back, digging her claws into me to keep me close. The slight bite of pain only increases the pleasure. I can feel how close she is, her breathing has become choppy and her walls are gripping me so tightly, I am not able to hold myself off any longer.

"Reach down and squeeze my knot, Angel. I want us to come together."

She follows my direction, taking my knot into her hand and gently applying pressure.

"Harder," I grit out.

Her hand clamps down hard, causing my eyes to nearly pop out of my head.

"Fuck!" I roar. "You are such a good girl, squeezing me so perfectly as I fuck your greedy pussy!"

Ramsey's body convulses, her walls locking down around my cock as I shoot my cum deep inside her.

I collapse on top of her, making sure to keep some of my weight off of her. We are both breathing heavy, covered in sweat, with huge smiles on our faces.

"Are you okay?" I ask hesitantly. I want her to be okay for many reasons—but that was the best sex of my life and I would very much like to do it again.

"I am great. No panic. No bad memories. Just us."

We hold on to each other for a long time. Ramsey falls back asleep with her head on my chest and my cum running down her legs. I could stay like this forever.

After Ramsey wakes again, we get dressed and leave our room in search of food.

"Oh shit," she says. "I forgot to get that tea from Heka."

"It's okay. We can pick some up from her today. We will need a large batch of it after the bonding anyway."

"I was going to drink some before we...it won't be too late, will it?"

"No, Angel. It will be okay. I have been drinking the tea anyway. We probably should have had this conversation before, but I didn't want you to feel pressured. I want everything with you—but I want to wait until we know each other a little better. I would like to have time with you before we add kids into the mix. Is that okay?"

"I want that too," she says shyly. "Though, I hear the tea might be a bit of a crap shoot with Ro around."

I chuckle as we enter the dining room. Everyone else is already there and they look up at us with knowing smiles as we walk in.

"Hey guys! Don't stop on our account," Ramsey says. When everyone continues looking at us, she asks, "What's up?"

I can hear War mumble, "Seems like Griff was," under his breath.

Rowan elbows him before saying, "Sit down, you must have worked up an appetite."

"Oh god. How do they know?" Ramsey whisper-yells at me.

Rowan replies, "Well, I know because you are all glowy. I'm guessing the wolves can smell him on you."

I am sure that Ramsey is going to run from the room with embarrassment. But instead, she shrugs and says, "It's a good thing he smells so delicious then," kissing me on the cheek before she sits down.

After a pause, the entire room breaks out in laughter.

Leaning close so that only I can hear, Ramsey whispers, "You totally wanted them to find out. That's why you didn't want us to bathe this morning."

I flash her a wicked smile in response because she is right. I want the entire world to know that she is mine.

After breakfast, Ramsey heads to the clinic with Rowan and Heka. She thinks that I am going to be working in the library, but really, I have some important errands to run before tomorrow. Sneaking out of the lodge, I make my way through the village to meet with the clothier and one of my best jewelers. In addition to the ceremonial cuffs that we will need, I have commissioned another piece from them.

Incredibly happy with their work, I stow the pieces away in the lodge and then meet with our staff who will be helping to make everything come together tomorrow night. Ramsey has been through so much already. I want tomorrow to be perfect for her.

Chapter Eleven

Ramsey

Walking back from the clinic, I reflect on how right my life feels at the moment. A young boy was brought in with a broken leg this morning. Shifters heal faster as wolves, but this little guy was refusing to shift. I was able to set the bone and then calm him down enough to shift. I then re-stabilized the leg in his shifted form, making sure that it would heal properly. It felt so rewarding to be able to help someone with skills that I had worked hard to learn. The irony of me wanting to become a veterinarian, finding work as a human nurse, and then being transported to a world where people are both human and animal is not lost on me. I really feel like I was meant to be here all along.

Now, I am lugging a hefty bag of tea leaves to our room so that we can dose ourselves often during the heat. I am a little nervous that we will forget, but Heka assured me that Griffin's wolf will remind him, knowing that we are not ready for any babies.

Rowan promised to keep her potent pussy powers on the other side of the lodge for the duration of my heat.

I still do not feel any magic within myself, like I did when I healed Ro. Heka believes that it will come back once the bond is sealed. As if the magic that I accessed was just a sneak peek of the power that I will have, and it was just triggered in that moment due to my heightened emotions.

I am not getting my hopes up, but I guess if there is someone we should trust, it is probably the lady who is almost 1000 years old.

It would be amazing if I was able to heal others though. Maybe I could save the babies and mothers who are lost far too often in childbirth. Or that kiddo from earlier today could have been healed immediately instead of feeling the pain of the break for any extended amount of time.

I am doing better around men. When the boy was brought in by his father today, I could feel my panic starting—but I focused my attention on the boy and was able to get through it.

I am able to be around War and Lycus without many issues. They still keep a respectful distance, but it is all getting better.

Logically, I know that I need to complete the bond with Griffin so that I can be stronger in a world filled with predators. But my heart wants the bond too. I want to bond myself to Griffin because it feels right. He feels right. Griffin is patient and kind. He does not treat my issues as a burden. With Griffin, I feel precious, like he will gladly make any accommodations if it means even the tiniest smidge of comfort for me.

As Alpha, I am sure he is supposed to bond in public, with his pack as witnesses. From what Ro said, she was not given another option. But he has agreed to have our ceremony be private. He was called back out to one of the outposts but because of the distance, he sent Dex instead. He did not want to be away from me at night, just in case I had a nightmare.

I feel supported in a way that I have never felt in my life. Even growing up, I was the one who took care of Rowan and Reese. I had to grow up quickly. I had to work multiple jobs. And I had to make sure we ate and went to school and had clean clothes. There was no other option—not if we wanted to stay together.

But here, I have Griffin. Here, *my* needs are met without question.

I feel supported. Accepted. Loved.

So, tomorrow I will bond myself to Griffin. We already share a soul; it makes sense that he has the rest of me as well.

I do not know what I did to deserve any of this, but I am so thankful that we have found each other.

When I fall asleep later that night in Griffin's arms, sweaty and sated, I do not fall into a dreamless sleep.

The cell is how it always is. Dank, dark, echoes of misery in the air. I hear footsteps approaching—but instead of fear, I feel safe. These footsteps are different, they beat to the sound of my heart, in tune with me down to my marrow. These footsteps belong to my Mate. Griffin enters my cell and scoops me up into his arms. I am too weak to walk on my own, so Griffin carries me out of Hell, tucked safely in his arms—and I never look back.

Chapter Twelve

I wake the next morning to an empty bed. I sit up, hoping that Griffin is just in the bathroom or reading in his chair, but he is nowhere to be found. Walking over to the small table, I see a steaming cup of tea and a note.

Drink me, then go into the bathroom for your next instruction.

Huh. I pick up the tea and slowly sip it, thankful that it has a pleasant taste, while I walk into the bathroom. I know that this is the birth control tea that I am going to be chugging over the next several days. Our ensuite bathroom is the biggest and the most luxurious in the whole lodge. I wouldn't be surprised if it is the best in all three territories. While the stone and glass finishes are beautiful, my favorite part of the bathroom is the very large hutch that houses soaps, salts, and oils. My next clue is tucked under Griffin's favorite soap.

Take a relaxing bath. Lather your delicious body in oils and then dress in one of my shirts. Rowan will arrive with your next instruction.

Chuckling to myself, I do as the note says. I take my time picking out the perfect scent combination before filling the tub with a bubble bath. I rub my body down in oils and wash my hair, working through all of the tangles. Griffin shaved me yesterday, so my skin is soft and smooth.

When the water starts to cool, I reluctantly drag myself out of the bath and throw on one of Griffin's shirts, smelling the collar, knowing that he wanted his scent on me.

A few minutes later, Rowan walks into the room with a tray of breakfast and my next note.

Eat me. I will eat you later tonight.

Ro waggles her eyebrows at me, clearly having read the note.

"I can't believe he is doing all of this," I say.

"I can. He is obsessed with you—as he should be. You deserve to have someone take care of you, you know?"

"I am a little nervous for tonight," I admit quietly. She raises her eyebrows in surprise, so I quickly add, "But not because it is Griffin. I just do not really know what to expect. You know that I am a planner."

Ro nods her head as she grasps my hand. "I think that you should just trust Griffin to have planned everything and let yourself enjoy it all. You *know* that he has used that big brain of his to think of every detail. It is kind of like a wedding but with less clothes and more biting."

I stuff a pastry into my mouth. The biting was mentioned but I kind of forgot about it until now.

"Does it hurt? The bite?" I know in my soul that Griffin would never actually hurt me. But I'm not sure how I will react to any type of pain.

"Just the quickest pinch, kind of like getting a shot, but then it is pure pleasure. The whole experience will make you try to jump his bones; it won't matter that his grandmother is watching."

I almost choke on my breakfast. "Lord, woman."

Ro cackles and then says, "Nobody knows this—well, except for War, but after we exchanged bites, I was so worked up. War shifted into his wolf so that he could run us to our love nest cave as quickly as possible, but I couldn't hold off long enough. I came all over his back."

Now it is my turn to laugh.

Once I have calmed myself back down, I pull her into a hug. "Seriously though, I am so happy. And I am happy that you will be here with me—just not too close." If only Reese could be here too. I remind myself that she is safe with Griffin's brother. I know that we could postpone the bonding until after she arrives at the lodge. If I asked him, Griffin would agree. But I don't want to wait any longer. I want to claim him just as much as he wants to claim me. This timing feels right—even if Reese can't be here to witness it.

"I promise we will all keep our distance," she says with a smile. "And it will just be family."

We eat all of the food off of the tray, which is quite impressive since it was completely loaded. Rowan hands me another note.

The garden is off limits until tonight. No peeking. Go with Rowan to The Hideaway for some relaxation. I have translated a "spicy" romance novel for

"It looks like we are going to be reading a dirty book in your Hideaway," I tell her.

"Yes, please! I found a whole section of romance books in the library before you arrived. I tried explaining the chili pepper scale to the boys, but I am not sure if they fully understood."

"Well, apparently Griffin has translated a spicy book for me."

Ro laughs. "That is amazing and so on brand for him. Here I thought he was spending all of his time in the library trying to figure out how our moon magic works but instead he was making sure that you have smut to read on your wedding day."

I follow Rowan through the lodge, doing my best not to peek at the flurry of activity going on in the garden. It really does mean so much to me that he has done all of this.

We both plop down on the comfy couch in The Hideaway, picking up the books with our names on them and giggling when we see that he has marked the spicy chapters, just in case we wanted to skip ahead to the good parts. He really did think of everything.

A couple of hours later, we are both laughing and I am feeling a little warm from a particularly hot scene. When I told Ro what was happening, she laughed and said, "Oh yeah, that feels great. I definitely recommend trying it."

I know she said that War has been willing to try everything but is there anything that they haven't tried? There were vegetables being used in addition to everything the MMC had packing.

"Hey, don't give me that look," she scolds. "When you are banging your soulmate several times each day, you have plenty of opportunities to get adventurous. And remember, if you are both into it—it's not weird." If that isn't a motto to live by, I don't know what is.

There is a knock on the door, and I know who it is based on the look on Ro's face. War peeks his head in and asks me if he can come in. I agree, of course, it is literally his house.

He brings us a tray for lunch as well as another dose of tea for me to drink.

"I'm not sure you will need more of this since Griff made you some this morning—but it will not hurt to have extra," he explains. "Oh, and this is for you." He delivers me another note.

War joins us for lunch, though he is mostly fussing over Ro and making sure that she eats enough. Then we head back to my bedroom to get ready. Honestly, we still have a couple of hours before it is dark enough for the ceremony to begin, and I'm not sure what we need to do that will fill that time.

Luckily, there is wine involved.

I make sure that I only have one glass, but man it was worth it. I am feeling a little anxious as we get closer to it being time. Only now, it has less to do with the ceremony, and everything to do with getting all worked up throughout the day. I *know* that I will be having a ridiculous amount of orgasms soon. The anticipation is killing me.

Prior to becoming intimate with Griffin, I had never come more than once during sex—if that. But I can't get enough of him. I almost come just from thinking about

Griffin's godlike body and knowing how skilled he is at using it.

Estelle and Heka pin up my hair in intricate braids and then pull out a wrapped gift for me to open, before leaving me to get dressed on my own. Rowan leaves too, needing to get herself dressed for the evening as well.

Secured to the top of the gift, is my final note.

I cannot wait to make you mine in every way—mind, body, and soul.

I had these items specially made just for you. I hope they will make you feel

comfortable during our ceremony. If these items do not work for you, please

just wear my shirt and find me in the garden.

I am honored to bond with you, no matter what you choose.

I will meet you under the moon.

Wiping the tears away from my cheeks, I tuck the note with all of the others on our little table. How did I get so lucky to be seen so clearly?

I unwrap the package to find four beautiful cuffs. Each is covered in jewels and intricate silver beading. Next, I pull out a gauzy robe with the same beading sewn in, creating a beautiful moon design, matching the markings on our hands. The last piece in the package is the most beautifully impractical thong that I have ever seen. It is high waisted, cut perfectly so that it will cover my brand while still keeping my body mostly bare.

I can't help but chuckle when I see it. Griffin actually made me underwear.

I get myself dressed in all of the pieces. I have cuffs around my wrists and ankles, the band of the thong covers my brand, and the robe—while technically see through—makes me feel covered as I walk out of our suite and into the garden.

The garden is beautiful. Rowan must have helped with the decorations, because the entire thing is overflowing with fluffy, white flowers that glow in the moonlight. I walk towards the center, feeling eyes on me but not really seeing anyone. I find Griffin, completely naked, standing in front of a flowered arch and looking up at the sky.

His eyes lock on mine as I approach. I suddenly feel braver than I had before and slowly take off the robe once I am standing in front of him.

"You are so beautiful, Angel," he says quietly to me.

My eyes rake over his exposed body, stopping to stare shamelessly at his incredible cock. I can feel slick heat between my legs.

Griffin must smell my arousal because he lets out a low moan.

I hear Rowan clear her throat, reminding me that we are not actually alone right now.

"Subtle," I say, loud enough for her to hear.

"Just trying to move this along so that you can get to the good part without his family watching," she replies.

I snort and Griffin offers me my favorite smile. A promise of more to come.

"Thank you for today," I tell him. "For everything that you planned and how you took care of me, without me even asking or knowing what I might need. I don't remember a time when I wasn't taking care of someone else. Even before we were removed from our parents' home when I was 8 years old, I was the one who made sure that my sisters were okay. I know what it is like to go without. I had to grow up too fast. But with you, I don't need to be that person. With you, I can trust that my needs are met because you put me above all else. With you, I feel safe, cherished, seen. I can't tell you how amazing that feels, but I hope that I can show you every day from now until forever. I love you, Griffin. I love you more than I ever thought was possible. And each day, I love you more."

Griffin leans down and captures my lips in a firm but sweet kiss.

"I love you too, Ramsey. I never thought that I would be lucky enough to find my True Mate. Part of the reason why is because it is uncommon these days, but mostly I did not think that it would happen for me because I have spent most of my life living through others in books. It is hard to find your soulmate when you do not leave the library. But then you stormed into the lodge, clearly afraid but brave enough to stand up to my brother as he growled and snapped his teeth at you. Knowing what I do now, it makes the strength that you showed in that situation completely extraordinary. I have read thousands of pages, looking for answers as to how you were pulled here to me, why we were Moon Touched, and what it all means. We may never find the answers that we seek, but I know with absolute certainty that you are mine just as much as I am yours. You were brought here because this is where you were always meant to be. By my side. Holding my hand. Letting me love you. Your strength encourages me to be strong *for you*. Your bravery makes me believe that I can take on the world *for you*. You are my muse—as much a part of me as the heart that beats in my chest. As vital as the air that I breathe."

Griffin gestures to someone, though I can't really tell who because my eyes are filled with tears.

Ro's hand reaches out between us, dropping something into Griffin's hand before scurrying away.

"Rowan told me that in your world, rings are given as a physical reminder of the promises made to each other." Taking my hand, he places a ring on my left ring finger. The center stone is a sapphire blue moon, and it is surrounded by tiny star shaped diamonds.

"This is beautiful, Griffin."

He returns my smile. "My promise to you, under this moon, is to always be there for you. Through the good times, and the bad. I will celebrate your joys and share the weight of your burdens. Whatever path we choose, we will walk together. Always."

Unable to form words, I throw my arms around Griffin's neck and pull his body to mine. I press my mouth to his and kiss him like I will die if I don't.

Pulling away, Griffin asks if I am ready for the bite. When I nod my head, he sinks his teeth into my neck. Heat radiates in my core, sending absolute need throughout my body. He pulls back, licking at my wound as I bite him in return. I clamp down hard until I taste blood. I can feel heat spreading, running down my arms and settling in my chest. I give his mark one lick, moaning as I feel him suck on my pulse point.

I am vaguely aware of people cheering as Griffin scoops me into his arms and runs into the lodge, not stopping until we reach our room. He kicks the door shut as he carries me to our bed.

"I need you," I whimper. "I need you so bad it hurts."

"I know, Angel. Let me make you feel better."

Griffin doesn't waste any time, positioning himself between my legs and spearing me with his cock. I scream at the feeling, not having time to adjust to his size.

"Are you okay?" he asks.

"Yes," I moan. "Please fuck me hard. We can go slow later."

And fuck me he does. Griffin grips my hips firmly as he slams into me over and over, hitting that spot I didn't even know existed before his giant cock introduced me to it. I am so close, I can feel my walls flutter around him.

"Are you going to take my knot like a good girl?"

An embarrassingly loud moan leaves my lips. I want nothing more than to be his good girl. "Please, Griffin. I need your knot," I beg.

Griffin growls into my neck, thrusting his knot into my pussy. I feel as my walls clamp down around him. As he locks us together, our orgasms wash over us in wave after wave. My vision goes black and the world around us ceases to exist. It is just Griffin and me, and the sounds of our ragged breaths.

Griffin shifts us so that I am sprawled out on top of him, still locked together. His fingers trace the lines of the moon markings on my hand as it rests on his chest.

"Do you feel any different?" he asks quietly.

"I feel forever changed," I reply. "I feel full. I feel whole."

Griffin brushes his lips across mine. It is a barely there kiss, but it feels infinitely significant.

"I feel the magic," I continue. "It's in my chest. Like it is filling a hole I didn't realize was there until now. And there is a warmth radiating from it, trailing down my arms and into my hands."

I remember what Ro had told me about how she learned how to communicate with War mind to mind. She told me that she had to search for the thread connecting them and then willed the door to open. When I look within myself, the line connecting me to Griffin is blazing, impossible to miss. There are not any doors or walls blocking the path. We knocked all of those down already. We are completely open to each other.

"And I can do this," I try.

"Clever girl," he replies sleepily.

"I love you, Griffin," I whisper.

"I love you too, Angel."

Chapter Thirteen

Griffin

I want to live between Ramsey's thighs. It has been five amazing days of absolute bliss and I do not ever want it to end. We can both feel her heat subsiding, though neither of us are in a hurry to leave our cozy bubble.

Our room reeks of arousal and sweat. Ramsey's honeysuckle and vanilla scent clings to the air, mixing with my own spicy scent beautifully. At this point, I am sure that the entire lodge smells of us. I am torn between being a possessive bastard, not wanting anyone else to experience her scent, and a proud brute, wanting everyone to know that I have this effect on her. That I have claimed her as mine. My instincts are in constant battle with my more sensible mind.

Ramsey has not had any nightmares—though she probably has not received enough sleep to allow one to take hold. She told me that her last nightmare changed. She no longer fears waking up in the cell because she knows that I would find her.

She is right. I would cross worlds to get to her and tear down anyone in my way.

I should probably let her sleep, but I cannot help myself. The depth of need that I feel for her is unreasonable. I now understand why War cannot keep his hands off of his Mate.

She had fallen asleep on my knot, so I slowly pull myself out of her dripping channel, licking my lips as I lower my face to soothe her tender cunt.

I slowly run my tongue through her center, healing her in the process. Now that she has some of my magic, she heals much quicker than she did before. But we have been having sex almost non-stop—that is a lot to keep up with.

I fuck my tongue in and out of her, lapping up our shared arousal. Her sweetness mixed with my saltiness is delicious. I moan at the taste.

Ramsey starts to stir, moaning and pushing her cunt towards my mouth. When she reaches down to grip my hair, I know that she is ready for more. She holds me against her pussy as I spear my thick fingers into her, curling them to hit that special spot that she hides inside.

"More," she begs. Her voice is a mix of a whine and a moan.

I smile against her clit.

Twisting my hand, I scissor my fingers inside of her, moving my thumb over her puckered hole.

She gasps.

"Has anyone ever touched you here, Angel?"

"No. But I want you to," she confesses. "I want you to claim me everywhere."

Fuck. A possessive growl rumbles in my chest, loving that idea.

I flip her onto her stomach, placing a pillow under her so that she is kneeling in presentation for me. I pull my fingers from her, moving them to rub circles on her clit while I lick my tongue through her entire crease.

Ramsey groans, arousal dripping down her thighs. Not wanting to stop my tongue from working her over, I speak directly into her mind.

"I will fuck your pretty ass, but we need to work up to it first."

"Yes, please," she replies.

I dive in, swirling my tongue around her asshole, getting it nice and wet before forcing my tongue into her.

"Fuuuuuck," she moans.

"Go ahead and come with my tongue in your ass."

Moments later, she detonates. Her body convulses, her cunt and ass pulsing around me.

"Good girl," I purr into her mind.

I keep working her over, extending her orgasm as she writhes in pleasure. Taking my cock in my free hand, I pull back and squeeze my knot, shooting my release all over her ass. Using my cum as lubricant, I gently push my finger into her ass, allowing the muscle time to open for me.

"Holy fuck, Griffin."

I set a steady rhythm with my fingers, pumping in and out of both holes until she is close to coming again. When I add a second finger to her ass, she screams out a release so wild that she completely floods the bed below her.

"You are so perfect," I praise, as I pull my fingers out, taking the ones that were in her pussy into my mouth.

Giving her a moment to breathe, I climb off of the bed and start a bath, adding in soaps and salts to soothe her wrecked body. I carry her to the tub, lowering us both down and holding her tight to my chest.

I gently wash her skin and her hair, wishing she could remain covered in me but knowing that she feels better when she is clean.

I massage her sore muscles and then grab the sharp knife that we keep by the tub and start shaving her. I work slowly as I glide the edge of the blade against her tanned skin. She is so relaxed in my arms; I try hard not to jostle her too much. Reaching my arm around, the knife slips from my hand, falling into the water. Ramsey jolts and I instantly know that it cut her.

"I am so sorry, Angel. Are you okay?" I pull her leg higher out of the water to check her over. The cut is not deep, but beads of blood well up at the surface. I reposition us so that I can reach her with my tongue, but she stops me.

"I want to try something first," she explains.

Ramsey holds one hand over her heart and the other over her wound. After mere moments, a silvery light flows from her hand and into her leg. She lifts her hand and reveals unblemished skin. The cut is completely gone.

"I did it!" she squeals, clapping her hands excitedly.

"How did you do it?" I ask, shocked. I run the pads of my fingers over her smooth leg. "It took Rowan a while before she could use her power with intention."

"Ever since our bonding, I have been able to feel small amounts of power traveling from my chest down to my hands. It is always there, like it wants to get out, but can't without me allowing it. I didn't know how to make it work, but I just trusted my magic to show me. All I needed to do was picture in my mind what my leg should look like without the cut and allow the power to leave my hands."

"You are incredible," I move her body flush with mine and kiss the top of her head.

"Thank god I studied anatomy and have all of those pictures locked into my brain. Do you think that the internal anatomy of wolf shifters is the same as it is in humans? I will have to learn wolf anatomy. Do you have any books I could check?"

I can feel her brain working in overdrive about all of the things that she might be able to do with her magic.

"I definitely have some books that can help, pretty girl. When your heat is fully over, we can head to the library."

"Will I be able to read them now? Without you translating them first?"

"I have not been speaking to you in your language since we bonded."

"Seriously? I couldn't even tell."

I lean in and give her a kiss, mostly because it has been several minutes since I had my mouth on her. I finish shaving her and then we make our way back to our bed, stopping to grab our meal tray from out in the hall. We are both in desperate need of some food and sleep.

The next day, the heat is officially over. We walk into breakfast, hand in hand, ready to tell our family the good news.

Being the last to arrive thanks to a delicious start to our morning, everyone looks up as we enter.

"Well, well, well look who the cat dragged in," Rowan says, a knowing smirk on her face.

"What did you call me?" Ramsey says, jokingly.

"I will happily follow your pussy anywhere," I whisper too loudly into Ramsey's ear.

Rowan and Ramsey both snort.

I quickly load up our plates while Ramsey hugs her sister and then I drag her into my lap.

"I can sit in my own seat, you know," she teases.

"It has already been too long since I have been inside you. Either you sit on my lap or we leave so I can fuck you," I whisper in her ear. Ramsey's cheeks turn crimson. I take a big bite of pastry and flash her a smile.

"So...how is everyone feeling?" Rowan asks.

"Wolfish," I reply. "Tired," Ramsey says at the same time.

"Just as expected, then," War says with a bark of laughter.

"I do have this sweet new magic though. Would you like a demonstration?" Ramsey asks, mischief dancing in her eyes.

When everyone voices their agreement, I pick up a knife from the table and stab it into my hand.

"What the fuck?" War shouts.

"Was that really necessary?" Ramsey shakes her head as she takes my bleeding hand in hers.

"There is no world in which I would have let you injure yourself for a quick show and tell," I firmly reply.

Ramsey scoffs, but pushes her magic into my wound, magically stitching my skin back together. I raise my hand for everyone to see.

"That is remarkable," Heka says with awe. Pulling my hand to hers to take a closer look. "Can you do this with anyone?"

"I think so," Ramsey says. "But it isn't like I have tried with anyone else. It is the same magic that I healed Ro with, I just didn't have access to the magic again until after we bonded. I accidentally got cut during the heat and healed myself with no issue. I do need to study wolf and shifter anatomy, but once I know what everything is supposed to look like, I think that I can mend anyone."

"We are going to head to the library to pull any anatomy books that I have. With Ramsey's eidetic memory, it should not take her long to pull what she needs from them," I explain.

"I have always been jealous of your brain, Rams. Hey, does this mean you could heal yourself if we get rid of that brand?" Rowan asks.

I can feel Ramsey tense at the reminder of her brand.

"Shit, sorry. I didn't mean to blab in front of everyone," Rowan apologizes.

"No, it's okay, Ro," Ramsey replies quietly. "I probably could."

I turn her face towards me.

"Is that something you want to do?" I ask mind to mind.

"Maybe. I hate that it is there, but it is also a part of me now. It is a reminder of what I have been through, what I have survived."

"You do not need to decide right now. Whatever you choose, I support you fully," I say as I pull her into a deep kiss. *"You are beautiful and strong, with or without the mark."*

"You guys are doing the whole mind to mind thing, aren't you?" Rowan asks.

Ramsey breaks our kiss, turning towards her sister to give her a shy nod.

"Speaking of the whole mind to mind thing," I say, "I have been wondering something. Are you ladies up for an experiment?"

"You know I love science," Ramsey responds eagerly.

"This is a different kind of science, though we are absolutely going to be doing that again later, pretty girl."

"I think science is..." War finishes his thought in a whisper to Rowan.

"Oh, that is definitely the science that they are talking about, Big Guy. We are pro-science over here too," she replies.

"Blessed Mother," my father mumbles under his breath.

"As I was saying," I start again, "I want Ramsey and Rowan to try to talk mind to mind. I do not know if it is possible, but seeing as how War, Bade, and I can speak through our connection, in theory, the magic that we shared with our Mates in combination with their own bond as sisters, could mean that they can too."

"Oh! I am game. Rams, open that pretty brain up for me."

Ramsey snorts. "You got it, Ro. Just let me know when you are coming."

"That's what she said," Rowan replies, causing them to erupt in a fit of giggles.

"Just wait until there is a third one here at the lodge," War chuckles.

"Have there been any updates on that situation? I was a bit preoccupied this week."

"From the last message I received, Bade and Reese were at one of his outposts. He didn't mention which one."

"I did not want to cause Rowan additional stress, but it sounds like Reese needed some time to recover. She was not in good shape when Bade found her."

"But she is doing okay now?" I do not want to keep anything from Ramsey, but if she hears that her sister is hurt, she will insist on going to her, and it is simply not safe to do that at the moment.

"Bade said that she was ill and had not been given food for quite some time before he found her. But she is doing better now."

I subtly nod my head.

"Are you girls making any progress over there?" By the look that Rowan is giving Ramsey over the table, it appears they are having more fun trying to make each other laugh than actually giving my experiment a solid try.

"Our minds won't meld," Rowan says with an exaggerated pout.

"I can find our connection. It is like it is missing a chunk out of it. I think we need Reese," Ramsey explains.

"That is possible. She wouldn't be able to connect to you without magic though. She would need to find her True Mate," I explain.

"Maybe she already has," War suggests.

"You think..."

"It would make sense," Ramsey says. "There are three of you and three of us."

"It would be kind of unfair if they weren't able to join our brother-sister Mate group," Rowan adds.

Ramsey snorts. "We are not calling it that. That sounds way too incestuous."

"You're right. People are already going to wonder with how close we are." Rowan agrees. "Bros and Hoes? Sisters and their Brother Misters?" Ramsey shakes her head at her sister. "I'll keep workshopping."

"Breakfasts around here sure have become more interesting," Heka says.

"People are going to talk anyway though, now that we have magic up the hoo-ha," Rowan continues.

"The only one going up your magic hoo-ha is me," War replies.

She smacks his arm. "Quiet, Big Guy. Little Mama is trying to think of a non-incestuous name for our Siblings in Love group that we have going on."

My father just stands up and leaves, causing the room to explode with laughter.

Chapter Fourteen

Ramsey

"Does your dad not like me?" I ask Griffin as we lay in bed later that night. "I feel like I made things so awkward between us when I first arrived."

Griffin turns my head so that he is looking into my eyes.

"He likes you," he reassures me. "Part of it is him trying to keep a respectful distance. I have not shared your past with him, though I am sure he suspects some of it."

"I don't mind if he knows," I tell him. "I just don't want anyone to only see me for what happened to me. Maybe I should talk to him. He shouldn't have to be walking on eggshells around me. Especially not in his house."

Griffin's hand rubs soothing circles on my back. "It is your home too. The lodge belongs to all of us."

"He just seems more open with Ro—and she is a bigger personality to get used to."

"The first time he met her, he had barged into War's room not realizing she was there. He definitely witnessed more than he intended."

I snort. Based on what I know about Ro's sex life, it could have been quite the eyeful.

Griffin pulls me closer and trails his fingers down my back while I rest my head on his chest. "My father lost a part of himself when my mother died. He has not been the same since—the lodge has not really been the same since. This has always been my primary residence, but War and Bade spent most of their time out in their territories. Being here was hard for all of us. But you and Rowan have breathed new life into all of us, and into this place. With the babies on the way, he worries for Rowan and War. He is keeping a closer eye on them because of what he experienced."

"I won't let anything happen to them," I interrupt.

"I know. And they do too. But it still brings those feelings of loss closer to the surface. My mother died giving birth to twins when my brothers and I were young. My father shut down after that, he refused to be Alpha. My uncle, his Beta, kept everything running until he was killed in an attack. That is when we became Alphas."

"I can't imagine how hard that was. It must have been a lot of responsibility to carry."

"I think that you carried more from a much younger age," he says.

"That might be true. But I didn't really grieve the loss of my parents. I understood that we were better off without them. And, while not all placements were ideal, I knew that my sisters had their basic needs being met— which was something I was not always able to do on my own. The hardest part for me was realizing that I couldn't be everything that they needed at the time."

"You were so young yourself. That was not something you should have had to deal with."

"I know that now. But I didn't know anything different back then. By the time Reese was born, our parents had already been lost to their addictions. One of our elderly neighbors would buy us groceries with the money that my parents left us for the week. That was one of the only things that they did for us—leave us a small amount of cash to get by while they were gone. But once Reese was born, the formula that she needed used up most of our cash. I was terrified to go to school. Most days, that meant leaving Ro to take care of Reese until I got back home. But we needed the food. There were many days that we only ate because of the food that I was able to take home from the lunch that was provided. I could see that other kids didn't live the same way that we did. Some of them even brough food from home to eat at school. But it was the only way we knew."

"And nobody did anything?"

I shake my head. "Not until I was 8 and had gone too many days without showing up to school. Both Reese and Ro were sick, and I needed to stay home with them. That is when we were placed in foster care."

"You are so strong," Griffin says, squeezing me a little tighter. "Even as a child, you were so strong."

We lay together in silence for a while. Before Griffin, I did not realize how much I needed someone who saw me. Who could truly see all that I am and have been going through. Someone who would take me as I am, flaws and all.

"I think that having Estelle here is hard for my father too," Griffin says as he continues our conversation from before.

"Because of your mom? They were twins, right?"

"Yeah. She looks almost identical to my mother. The only real difference is her eyes. Mother's eyes were the same blue as ours."

"I never pressed because I was going through my own shit, but she seemed so lonely at her cottage. She moved around like a ghost. Maybe it will be good for both of them to be here and experience life again."

Griffin pauses before he speaks. "I think you are right, Angel. But I am sure it will not be long before she returns to her home. I have invited her to stay here many times and she has never accepted the offer. It is something that she will need to decide to do on her own." I feel the press of Griffin's lips against my temple. He lingers for a while, lost in thought.

Before long, I let sleep pull me under. Snuggled up against my Mate, I dream of the future my new life could hold.

We are awoken to the sounds of Ro rushing into our room, War hot on her heels.

Startled, Griffin growls and pulls me under his large body.

"Love, I told you to let me wake him up first. Griff, put your teeth away," War grumbles.

Griffin makes sure that my body is covered with a blanket before getting out of bed to find us some clothes. War quickly covers Ro's eyes at the sight of my Mate's naked body.

"Sorry to invade your love nest," Ro says, "but we have been called out to a difficult delivery, and I was hoping that you might be able to help with your sweet healing powers."

"Oh! Of course," I say as Griffin slips one of his shirts over my head before pulling some pants on himself.

"You can bring your genius with a penis. There is no way War will let me go anywhere without him again," she adds.

I snort. Genius with a penis.

"I am definitely coming," Griffin responds, stowing the anatomy books that I was studying before bed into a bag. "Which pack?"

"Nightfury," War responds.

Moments later, we are out the door and heading to my first delivery in this new world. I have seen several patients at the lodge but have not felt comfortable heading out into the village. There are too many triggers. But, with a purpose in front of me and Griffin's hand in mine, I know that I can do this.

We approach the house and before we enter, my nose twitches at the smell of blood in the air.

"Do you smell that?" I ask Griffin quietly.

He gives me a nod. "I am surprised that you do, though. It seems you got a little more from me when my magic transferred over."

We are greeted at the door by a large male. I immediately step behind Griffin and take deep breaths. I can't afford to let my fear take hold if I am going to help the laboring mother inside.

"I was not expecting Alphas," the man says gruffly. I can't tell if he is always this grumpy or if he is upset that we are the ones who answered the call.

"Where they go, we go," War replies. "Is that going to be a problem?" The man shakes his head before gesturing us inside.

Ro and I are sandwiched between our Mates as we walk through the house to the back bedroom. I was expecting to find a pool of blood given how heavy I scent it in the air, but it is not as bad as I thought. The mother is not quite ready to push. We still have time.

"Do you know how many you are expecting?" Ro asks.

The woman shakes her head. "I have been too afraid to have someone check," she confesses.

Ro turns to War, who immediately kneels with his ear close to the woman's belly.

"Two," he says.

The father curses and the mother's eyes fill with tears.

"It is going to be okay," I say. Griffin pulls out one of the books that he brought with, flipping to the drawn image of a twin pregnancy to refresh my mind. I haven't read that far so I appreciate his forethought.

I am unsure how much to tell this family about my powers. We had discussed keeping it quiet until I had practiced more, but it seems The Mother had other ideas.

"Can you ask War to take the father out of the room?" I ask Griffin.

Griffin nods and after giving Ro's shoulder a squeeze, War escorts the man out of the room in search of clean linens.

"I am a trained nurse," I tell the mother. "But I also have Moon Touched magic. It allows me to heal." I show her the shimmery silver moon tattoos that cover my hands.

"She saved me and my babies when we were attacked," Ro adds.

"I am going to do everything that I can to make sure you and your babies survive this birth, okay?"

Other than when I healed Ro, I have never had to use my powers for something like this. I suspect it will require a bit more magic than I used to heal my cut and Griffin's hand. Taking one more thorough look at the picture Griffin is holding out for me, I close my eyes and push my magic out of my hands.

Not totally knowing what I am looking for, I look for any differences instead. It is kind of like a strange 'Where's Waldo' as I compare what my magic is seeing versus what the picture depicts. After several minutes, I found it. A small tear in the uterine wall. I can see it in my mind as my magic stitches it closed.

The entire room is quiet when I open my eyes. Everyone is staring at me with looks of awe.

"I mended the complication. This should be a normal vaginal twin birth now," I explain.

When nobody says anything, I ask, "Why is everyone looking at me like that?"

"You just turned into a full-on glow worm, Rams," Ro explains.

"My hands always glow when I use my magic," I say, still confused. They have seen me use my magic before.

"You had light coming out of your eyes too, Angel," Griffin replies.

"Huh," I say. "I did need to use more of my magic. It was like I could actually see inside her body. It is how I was able to find the tear."

"That is incredible," Griffin replies in awe, kissing my temple.

"Are you feeling okay?" I ask the mother. I do not like all of the attention on me and really, this situation is about her.

"It feels like the worst stomach cramps I have ever had along with the pressure of a boulder trying to push its way out of me," she replies.

"Right on schedule, then," I reply with a smile.

"This is my first labor," she admits quietly.

I take her hand in mine. Labor is a vulnerable time for even the most experienced mothers.

"That's okay," I tell her. "This might be your first time, but I have helped deliver hundreds of babies. It is okay if you are nervous or scared, but just know that I'm not, okay?"

The mother nods, sucking in a breath as another contraction starts.

Griffin and Ro are looking at me like I just said something groundbreaking. I just learned quickly during my training that most patients just need to know that they are not alone.

"Hey, Sweets," I look up at Griffin. He smiles at the nickname.

"Yes, pretty girl?"

"The rest of this process is pretty straight forward. Ro and I can handle it. Can you go hang with War and the father, give this mama some privacy?"

"Of course," he replies with another kiss on my head. "I will be right outside. Let me know if you need anything."

Within an hour, the mother is ready to start pushing. Ro lets me take the lead, supporting me while I talk the mother through the deliveries. Once the babies are out, Ro takes them to the side, cleaning them up a bit before handing them to the mother.

One of the babies was born in his wolf form, which wasn't something I was expecting, but everyone is healthy. Two boys. I take a breath and let this moment sink in. The first set of multiples born alive in over 100 years. There is no doubt in my mind that news of this birth will travel fast. I just hope that it results in support and not fear of this incredible magic that I have been blessed with.

Ro and I clean the mother up before calling the guys back in. We are thanked profusely—the father even tried to pull me into a hug. When I backed away, Ro swooped in and accepted it for me.

Whether it is from the magic that I used or the stress of the situation, I can feel my energy begin to crash as we head out the door. Griffin lifted me into his arms to carry me.

"I am so proud of you," he whispered in my ear. I snuggle closer, burying my face into his neck. I am fast asleep before we make it back home.

Chapter Fifteen

The next week passed without much incident. There was one delivery that I assisted with, but it was a standard single delivery. Both mother and child made it through without the need for my magic.

In the next month, we are going to start experiencing the deliveries of the pregnancies that were influenced by Ro's magic. From what I was told, most are multiples. I am going to do everything that I can to be available for those mothers when it is time.

But first, I am heading out with Griffin to a few of his outposts. He has been avoiding making the trip due to the distance, but we have been reassured that the threat of Dreena's supporters is no longer present within Nighthowl territory. Her entire operation seems to have fled to Nightfury and even across the borders into the panther and bear territories.

Our goal is to be back in two weeks.

I am nervous to leave the lodge but I know that I will be safe and supported by Griffin. My nightmares have not returned and as long as unknown men keep some distance, I can stop panic attacks before they fully take hold.

Dex, Griffin's Beta, will be traveling with us, as well as a small group of Bade's soldiers. I have met Dex before and he keeps a respectful distance. Griffin gave him the Cliff Notes version of my experience. I was hesitant to share, but we ultimately decided that everyone traveling with us should be aware of my triggers. And while Dex does look at me a little differently, it is not with pity. The soldiers that Griffin selected are all females who were living and working within the village. I will officially meet them once we arrive at our first stop this evening— though they will be running alongside us in their wolf forms.

The fact that he thought about my comfort while still prioritizing safety means more to me than he will ever know.

We will be traveling light, using items that Griffin keeps stashed at outposts along the way and picking up anything else that we might need from vendors throughout the territory. I packed a small bag with some dresses, knowing that I will just sleep naked or in Griffin's shirt while we travel.

Rowan offered me a pair of leather pants to help prevent my thighs from being rubbed raw, but I will just heal myself if it becomes an issue. Nighthowl territory is along the southern expanse of wolf land. We are beginning the warmer months and it will only get hotter as we travel. The thought of pulling on a pair of pants sounds miserable. I have even started wearing the bralettes that Ro favors, pairing them with a high waisted, flowy skirt that covers my brand.

I am not sure if my body image will ever return to what it used to be, but it is improving. Griffin helps me a lot with that. When he looks at me, he sees strength. I want to see that too. It has taken a lot of processing, but I am starting to see all of my scars, internal and external, as a symbol of my survival instead of damage. I still get embarrassed when I have a panic attack, but those are happening less and less too.

I say my goodbyes to everyone, making sure to privately thank Estelle for her help in my recovery and journey here. Just like Griffin predicted, Estelle will be heading back to her cottage shortly after we depart. She promises to return for visits, especially once the babies are born, but she needs more time to heal before she is able to commit to living at the lodge. I understand that. We are all on our own journeys.

A few moments after I make my way to the entryway, Griffin's massive wolf barrels into the room, skidding to a halt at my feet. I lean in, giving him a hug while he lays a wet lick on my cheek.

"Hey, Sweets," I say. "I probably should have asked how this all works."

Ro shouts from the landing, "Just spread your legs for him and enjoy the ride!"

I snort. "So just a typical Friday night then, huh?" Ro giggles with me and then I turn to my Mate. "Okay, let's do this."

Griffin licks my face again. I'm sure that he is intimidating to most. He is huge, even compared to the few wolves that I saw from a distance on my trip here with Estelle, but with me he is far more similar to a golden retriever.

I stand up, with my legs slightly parted. In one smooth motion, Griffin crouches down behind me and scoops me up onto his back. After giving me a moment to stabilize myself, he takes off, leaping through the front door of the lodge and down into the busy streets of the village.

Looking behind me, I see the others that have fallen in line to follow us. I count six wolves. One large wolf has black fur and golden brown eyes—that has to be Dex. I have never seen his wolf form but his hair and eyes are the same shades. The other five wolves are slightly smaller and fan out to make a semi-circle formation around us. I am amazed by how cohesively they work together, adjusting themselves around obstacles that we pass on our way out of town.

It takes about a half hour to make it through the village, leading out to the sparsely populated outskirts of Nighthowl territory.

"Did you name your territory or was it always named Nighthowl?" I ask.

"My brothers and I named our packs. Before we took over, the wolves were split into the three territories, but the entire pack resided under the name of Night."

"What made you choose Nighthowl?"

"My beautiful singing voice."

I crack up laughing. I'm sure that I look like a lunatic to anyone around.

"You laugh, but it is partly true," he continues. *"Bade chose Nightfury because his wolves are responsible for our military. He wanted something that would reflect strength. War chose Nightfang because they are our hunters."* Griffin snapped his teeth for emphasis, making me giggle. *"Nighthowl is made mostly of artists, in one form or another. We add beauty back into our lives. A wolf's howl is really just a song for those who take the time to listen."*

"That is beautiful, Griffin. Unfortunately for you, I couldn't carry a tune in a bucket."

I hear his laugh in my mind, loud and free. I allow it to settle into my soul. *"That is okay. I will carry it for you,"* he replies.

We traveled for the rest of the day, stopping only when I had to pee and to have a quick lunch. We fill our time with chatting about our siblings and what it was like living in New York.

Just as the sun is about to set, we arrive at our stop for the evening. Estelle and I never stopped at an outpost on our journey, so I am seeing the set up for the first time.

This outpost is large. From what I was told, Dreena had a stronger influence over the smaller outposts as she worked her way through the territories gathering support. With the exception of one stop, we will be sticking to the larger outposts along our journey. There are several yurt style buildings in varying sizes. One of the larger structures is clearly a central kitchen and dining area, the delicious smells of cooked meat and fresh bread flow freely from the open doors. There is a large central fire with seating next to the dining area.

Thirty or so smaller structures radiate out from there in an organized pattern. Several of these homes have outdoor workspaces attached, holding supplies for the different crafts and wares that they create. One has a beautiful tapestry depicting the full lunar cycle with stars so shimmery that they almost glow. I have no idea what material the artist used to create the stars, but it is breathtaking.

We catch everyone's attention as we make our way through the village, but nobody stops us. Our group slowly peels off, pairing up as they pass their lodgings for the evening. Griffin told me that there are plenty of open homes to accommodate our small group, so they each get their own space.

Griffin takes me into his lodging, which is positioned towards the back of the village and is slightly bigger than the homes that we passed on our way here. Once inside, Griffin shifts, reaching around to hold me so that I do not fall.

He chuckles at my surprised gasp and then plants a sloppy kiss on my mouth, making me squeal.

"A little warning before you pull that move would be nice," I say.

"Just trying to keep you on your toes," he replies with another kiss. "Food will be here soon. Are you hungry?"

I nod my head, biting down on my bottom lip while I take in his beautiful naked body. Riding on his back all day has worked me up in a way that I did not expect. From the look of his massively hard cock, he could use some relief too.

"I think that I might be overdressed for the meal I am hungry for," I say, peeling my dress up over my head and dropping to my knees.

Up until this point, I have been nervous to take him into my mouth. I know that it has a good chance of triggering me. But I want this with him. I don't want there to be anything that we can't do with each other. We have never talked about it directly, but I have shared most of my experiences with him and he has never suggested that I try. He follows my lead whenever we are trying something new. Always willing and never pushy. If I didn't already know that he was my soulmate, the way that he is exactly what I need is proof enough.

Looking down at me, he gently places his hand on my cheek. "Are you sure, Angel?"

"Yes. I trust you," I reply verbally. I know that he needs my words.

I open my mouth. My tongue darts out to lick up the bead of precum already dripping from his cock. I moan at the salty, spicy taste of him. Holding the weight of him in my hand, I slowly take him into my mouth. He is so large, it would be impossible to fit his entire length, but I add my hand at the base of him, working in as much as I can until he hits the back of my throat—making myself gag.

Griffin stays completely still—if it wasn't for his heavy breathing and the curse words escaping his mouth, I might not believe he is enjoying it.

I work my mouth over his length several times before grabbing his ass and pulling him deeper, encouraging him to move how he likes to.

"Does my good girl want me to fuck her mouth?" he says with a low growl.

I pull my mouth away so that I can reply, jacking him off with my hand to keep the rhythm going.

"Please," I beg, "I will be so good for you."

"You are so fucking good, baby. You were made to take my cock." Pushing back into my mouth, Griffin thrusts in and out of my mouth, hesitant at first but more sure with each stroke. My eyes water each time he hits the back of my throat, but I am so lost in lust I couldn't care less. He wipes my cheeks before working his hand into my hair, angling my head so that he fits even more of himself down my throat.

Wetness is pooling at my thighs and running down my legs. We can both smell my arousal, and I honestly think that I might be able to come just from this. I love the care he shows while taking what he wants from me.

"You are such a good girl," he tells me. "Are you going to swallow my seed down that pretty little throat of yours?"

I apply pressure to his knot as I moan. I need his release like I need air.

Right before he spills into my mouth, he reaches down and clamps my nipple hard between his fingers. It is enough to push me over the edge—my body convulsing as I swallow him down.

"You are so perfect, Angel," Griffin tells me as he picks me up and carries me to the bed. Without any warning, he dives between my legs, licking up my release and working my sensitive clit until another orgasm charges through me.

He works his way back up my body, leaving a trail of nips and kisses on his path to my mouth. Griffin takes my mouth with his. Our tongues lashing each other in a frenzied but deep pull. Our kiss begins to slow but instead of pulling away, Griffin positions the head of his cock against my entrance, pushing in slowly.

I squirm as I try to accommodate his size. I love the way he stretches me into the perfect fit. Our lovemaking is slow, steady. Each thrust brings us closer and closer to heaven. Griffin's teeth scrape down my neck and I feel my walls sucking him in. After a few more thrusts, he pulls my peaked nipple into his mouth, his fingers work my other in time with his tongue.

I grip his ass with my hands, forcing his knot into me on the next thrust. We both shatter, screaming each other's names as the world around us disappears.

I wake up the next morning feeling deliciously sore. After we ate some actual dinner and then bathed, we fell into bed where Griffin had me two more times throughout the night. I don't know if it is the whole soul bond thing or just us, but we cannot get enough of each other. I have been guzzling down Heka's birth control tea, not wanting to take any chances.

Back in New York, I was on the pill and always used condoms with my hookups. Between taking care of my sisters and working at the hospital, I did not have the time or the energy for a relationship, let alone another mouth to feed. Sex was purely a needed release. No feelings, no risks, no attachments. Truthfully, most of my orgasms were a result of my own hard work with a vibrator. When I explained what sex toys were to Griffin, he got a mischievous gleam in his eye. It is not something that they have here—not that I need it. Griffin keeps me well and truly satisfied.

Deciding I should get up for the day, I stretch and put on some clothes. Griffin left earlier to meet with some members of his pack. I quickly wash my face and brush my teeth before leaving our temporary home. One of the soldiers who are traveling with us met me at the door.

"Good morning!" I greet her. "I didn't get a chance to meet you properly earlier. What is your name?"

"Good morning, Alpha," she replies. I am thrown by the term. Griffin had explained that being his True Mate granted me the title of Alpha, but this is the first time someone has called me that. "My name is Briar. My twin sister Bree is in our group as well."

"It is really nice to meet you. You can call me Ramsey."

She looks like she is going to argue but nods her head anyway.

"I was hoping that we could track down some breakfast," I tell her, walking towards the kitchen area that I saw last night.

"We can definitely do that," she replies as she steers me to take the most direct path towards the communal kitchen. "The Alpha is meeting with some of his wolves in the dining area. I am sure he would be pleased to see you."

I feel a blush creep up to my cheeks thinking about the state in which he last saw me. "Yes, I'm sure he would," I agree. "Have you always been a part of the Nightfury pack?" I know that wolves can transfer to the other packs if approved by the Alphas.

"No, actually. My sister and I transferred to Nightfury from Nighthowl. Our parents are still a part of this pack. It is one of the reasons we were interested in coming on this trip. We will be stopping at their outpost in a few days."

"You must be excited to see them. How long has it been?" I am being nosy, but I want to get to know people. Back in New York, I was almost always surrounded by people. It has been so long since I have interacted with anyone outside of our family. If she is uncomfortable with my questions, she doesn't show it.

"It has been a few years since we have been home. But as long as we are not pulled away for a mission, we see our parents in the big village when they come to sell their pottery."

We step into the dining tent and Griffin's eyes immediately look up to lock with mine. I give him a smile and a little wave but follow Briar over to the food. It is not long before I feel his strong arms wrap around me from behind. He presses a quick kiss to my neck.

"Sleep well?" he asks, already knowing the answer.

"Very. Staying up to do all of that science really wore me out."

He throws his head back in a laugh, brushes a quick kiss to my lips, and then walks back over to continue his meeting.

"Make sure you get enough to eat, Angel. You will need the energy for later."

I continue to fill my tray and try to ignore the way that my core is pulsing at the promise of later.

I sit down at a table with Briar, and I am introduced to Bree, Ebony, and Idra. Dex is in the meeting with Griffin and Tane is patrolling the perimeter of the outpost.

"What made you decide to join the Nightfury pack?" I ask, continuing our conversation from before.

Bree is the one who replies. "We are only a year older than the Alphas. So, we were born when the pack was still Night but in the area that became Nighthowl. When we were 16, our cousin was killed in an attack at the border. She was there to trade. We decided that we wanted to make ourselves strong—able to defend ourselves and those we love. So, we trained as soldiers. It took a couple of years, not having lifted a blade or ever fought against another prior to this decision. Once we were strong enough, we approached Alpha Bade and he allowed us to transfer into Nightfury."

I want that too, I realize. Not to become a soldier, but to make myself strong, confident, and powerful. "Will you teach me?" The words are out of my mouth before I have a chance to second guess them. "I can't fight like a wolf. But can you teach me how to defend myself as a human?"

All four sets of eyes stare at me in slight shock. I am sure that they were not expecting it. I was not expecting it either. But it is something that I really want—maybe even need.

"Before I came here, to this world, I was in a horrible situation. I do not want to ever feel powerless again," I explain quietly.

"Will the Alpha be okay with it?" Idra asks.

"Yes." I say with certainty. Griffin will support anything that I want to do.

They exchange some looks back and forth before smiling.

"We will not go easy on you," Ebony explains.

"I don't want you to," I reply. "I need to be confident in protecting myself if the need ever arises again."

"Then we will teach you," Bree says.

"You will need some different clothing, unless you want to just go without. Skirts will get in the way," Briar explains.

"She will have whatever she needs," Griffin says as he walks toward us.

"We will start with morning runs and then some self-defense, working our way up to the more technical skills. If we are traveling, you can run alongside us for at least some of the time. It will be a good way to increase your endurance and build the muscles that you will need," Bree decides.

"Sounds like a good plan," I reply. I am excited to get started.

Chapter Sixteen

My limbs feel like they are on fire. We are on day five of my self-defense lessons and I am really starting to question if my idea was brilliant or just plain stupid. The first day of travel, the day after we came up with this idea, my instructors had me run next to them for about 20 minutes at a time. After 20 minutes, Griffin would scoop me up and carry me for about an hour before it was time to run again. We did that cycle four times before Griffin decided it was enough for the day and refused to put me back down.

I know that I am being hard on myself but when I lived in New York, I ran almost every day. I could run for miles at a time and even thought about signing up for a half or whole marathon but did not have the time to train properly.

But here, I can barely keep up. I could blame it on the fact that I do not have proper running shoes. I had to choose between my leather boots or going barefoot like everyone else. I have tried both and ended up with blisters or cuts on my feet either way. Luckily, I can just heal myself. I could probably heal my sore muscles too, but I promised myself that I would put in the work and retrain my muscles the old-fashioned way.

Griffin had several pairs of shorts made for me. I had briefly described what I usually wore to work out in, and he worked with a clothier in the outpost to quickly whip up some options for me.

In addition to running, I work with Briar and Bree on self-defense. They talk me through different scenarios and then show me how to get out of them. I am getting more confident with that each day.

After traveling all day, Griffin let me know that we are nearing our next stop. I ran with our group for the first hour of our journey this morning, and then another hour after we stopped for lunch. Exhausted, my trainers took pity on me and allowed me to ride for the remainder of the day.

This is the outpost where Briar and Bree's parents live. I am happy that my friends will get to spend time with their family and am even happier that I will get a small break from training. I know that I asked for this—and I really, truly need it—but these Fury ladies were not kidding when they said that they would not take it easy on me.

"I have a hot bath waiting for us when we get to our lodgings," Griffin tells me as we enter the outpost.

I groan at the thought of sinking my sore muscles into some hot water. Griffin's wolf chuffs—a sound that I now know is his laugh.

I wave at Briar and Bree as they split off from the group. Tane, Ebony, and Idra all find their lodgings while Dex takes the first watch.

Griffin takes us to his lodging, walking straight through the door and catching me as he shifts. I know that I should expect it at this point, but it surprises me every time. I'm sure he does it just to mess with me. There has to be a more practical way for me to dismount.

He carries me in his arms and kisses me soundly as we get closer to the bathtub. Testing the temperature of the water first, he adds a bit of cold water before stripping me down and lowering me into the tub. Griffin opens up a small cabinet and selects some bath salts and soaps before joining me in the water.

We sit and soak for a while. Griffin has his arms wrapped around me from behind, massaging my sore muscles as he fills me in on what he has to meet about tomorrow. Apparently, there is quite the town drama happening at this outpost. It sounds very Romeo and Juliette—two competing families trying to keep their children apart. The children claim that they are True Mates, but their families do not want them to bond under the full moon that is happening in a couple of days.

"What are you going to do?" I ask.

"I am going to meet with the couple and if they are truly True Mates, then I will grant them permission to bond. They are only 16 but have felt the pull of their souls since they first met years ago."

"Does that happen often? True Mates finding each other at such a young age?"

"It can. The pull can happen with kids. Or even an adult and a child. If that happens, their relationship is obviously different from the one that we share. A bond is never completed with a child. But, 16 is old enough to decide. My brothers and I were only 17 when we became Alphas. If I had found you at that age, I would have bonded with you."

"So, if someone your age meets a child who is their True Mate, what happens?"

"Usually, the adult would become a part of the family. Or more like a family friend. It depends a bit on the situation. The child's parents remain the primary caregivers. But they would need to live near each other. Interact with each other. Their wolves would not allow for them to be separated, but it is more of the role of a protector. The relationship is not inappropriate. They would never do anything to endanger their Mate."

"And then when the child is an adult, their relationship shifts?"

"Usually. But not fully until the bond is sealed. And only if and when both wolves want and are ready for that. Some might choose not to seal the bond and remain in that protector relationship. They would never find another to love, though. Once our wolves find their Mate, it is impossible to be with anyone else."

"Hopefully the families will support them once they have bonded," I say, thinking about the 16-year-old lovebirds.

"If they do not, I will encourage them to move to a different outpost or the big village. It is not worth the stress. True Mate bonds are sacred to us. They should be celebrated, not kept apart."

After our bath, Griffin finds us some dinner and then we fall into bed.

"Can I be at the meeting with you tomorrow?" I ask quietly. I have not attended any meetings with him so far on this trip. I am still nervous around men, and I usually take that time to work on self-defense exercises.

He responds with a smile. "Of course," he says.

I snuggle closer into his side. Griffin rubs my back in soothing circles.

"Thank you for bringing me with you," I say. "I wasn't sure if I was ready, but I think that I needed this. I needed a reason to leave the safety of the lodge so that I could see that the world outside isn't as scary as I remember."

"You are always safe with me."

"And I think that it will be good for me to help advocate for the True Mates tomorrow. Finding you has been the best thing that has ever happened to me. My life would have been hopeless if I hadn't passed out and woken up in this new world."

"Is that how it happened?"

I take a deep breath. Griffin knows that I have the brand, but I haven't told him any details about how it happened.

"Ro told me that she had been running and then she felt sharp static, then pain. When she looked up, War's wolf was standing in front of her." Griffin nods. "It was different for me." I take another steadying breath. "I was dragged from my cell. It was different from other times because other women were pulled out at the same time. They usually kept us apart and blindfolded when they took us from our cells. But not this time. The other women were completely strung out on the drugs they forced us to take."

I can feel the tears already soaking my cheeks. Griffin keeps a steady arm around me. He understands that I need to share this last piece. I need to set it free from my chest.

"They brought us into a larger room where men in suits drank and smoked around the edges. There were probably 30 of them. There were six of us. I am not sure if we were the only six left or if they were moving us in groups. I thought that they were going to sell us or something—and maybe they were—but before that happened, they made us kneel in the center of the room. They chained our hands to the floor and put gags in our mouths. I was so weak, there was nothing that I could do to stop it. One by one, the women kneeling with me began to scream and the smell of burnt flesh filled the air. I tried to block it all out—but I couldn't. All I could do was wait for my turn. That's when I got my brand. I think I was the last one. I must have passed out from the pain because when I became aware again, I woke up in Estelle's cottage. She told me that she found me when she was out foraging. I was naked, unconscious, and bleeding. She cleaned me up, gave me time to recover, and never asked what happened."

Griffin tucks me impossibly closer to his body. I melt into him and breathe in his scent while my tears continue to fall.

Opening up these wounds while I am safely wrapped in my Mate's arms is cathartic. The painful memory is purged from my soul. I am forever changed by it, but I do not need to carry the weight of it anymore. I am here. I am safe.

I bring my hand up to Griffin's cheek and pull his lips to mine.

Chapter Seventeen

Griffin

I wake up as the sun is just starting to rise. My body is completely entangled with Ramsey, her dark hair a wild mess across her pillow. She looks so peaceful as she sleeps. Her rosy lips, still swollen from my kisses.

Hearing her cry and the painful memory that she shared last night gutted me. I wish I could reverse time and stop it all from happening to her. I am in awe of her strength. I am so incredibly proud of how she has overcome such pain.

I do not want to disturb her peace, so I keep her tight against my body as I think about what the day ahead will bring. We will be staying at this outpost for one more night before traveling to the last outpost tomorrow and then start our journey home.

At each stop we have made so far, I have helped settle small disputes as well as ensured that everyone has what they need for the upcoming months. Many in my pack travel this time of year. However, due to the unrest that was caused by Dreena as she passed through, travel has been limited. Interruptions in travel caused interruptions in trade. Without proper trade, food has been more limited than I would typically like. There is still enough. Nobody is starving. But it has made everyone a little more on edge.

I think that is probably what has escalated the issue on the docket today. Both families involved are jewelers—very good ones at that. These families have always been competitive with each other, but with enough demand throughout the packs, it has never really been a problem. With travel and trade being limited, both families are feeling the strain, leaving these Mates in the middle.

Hopefully the families will be able to see the truth that True Mate bonds are inevitable. There is truly no stopping the pull of their souls once they have found each other. Both wolves will go mad if they are not able to be together.

I do not think that this meeting will become violent, but I want to make sure Ramsey feels supported so I reach out to Dex.

"Ramsey will be at the meeting this morning. Can you ask Idra, Ebony, or Tane to be in attendance too?"

"Of course. Tane is scheduled for watch so it will be Idra and Ebony."

"Any other updates?"

"There is one mother due to have her pup soon. The healer has requested that Ramsey sits in on the appointment this afternoon. Word has spread about her involvement in the successful twin birth."

"I will attend with her. We need to keep an eye on the situation and make sure that we shut down any threats. Dreena could still have supporters here."

"I agree."

"Our next stop is close to the border. I would like two guards with her at all times."

I feel his affirmation. We knew that word about Ramsey's powers would spread. A successful twin birth after over 100 years of loss is a big deal. Big enough that it might pull Dreena out of hiding in order to start another witch hunt.

I received word from Bade that he and Reese were on the move, making their way back to the lodge. Dreena was able to evade him. He believes that she has been crossing into bear and panther territory. He is not willing to risk Reese by following after her, so he is bringing Reese to safety while his Beta, Boone, tracks her down.

Reese is still having waves of sickness. Maybe Ramsey will be able to help her once we are all back at the lodge.

Ramsey starts to stir beside me. She does the cutest little stretch before opening her eyes.

"Good morning, Angel," I say softly. "Did you sleep well?"

"I slept great," she replies. "I always do when you are next to me."

"Then I will always be next to you," I tell her with a smile. "But right now, I am dying to be *in* you."

She giggles, spreading her legs to make room for me. I capture her lips with mine, pulling her sleepy moans out of her body. I kiss a trail down her body. Her neck, her chest, her taut nipples, her navel. I want to map every inch of her skin with my tongue. Hours spent in the warm sun has darkened her skin into a tanned glow. Freckles have started to appear on her cheeks, nose, and shoulders. Yesterday I counted 32. I wonder if she has gained any more.

"I had something made for you—for us."

"What is it?" she asks.

"I will show you in a little while. Let me get you ready first."

I slide down between her legs, teasing her thighs with kisses and bites, before swiping my tongue through her center. I moan as her taste explodes on my tongue. She is so sweet and delicious, I cannot get enough.

I spend a good amount of time working her up before pulling back away. I know that the more that I edge her towards release, the bigger her orgasm will be. And I need her dripping for my surprise.

When she comes, she gushes. My face is coated in her honey and I happily lick it off of my lips. I flip her over, continuing to eat her sweet pussy while I stroke myself. After she screams her second orgasm into her pillow, I know that it is time.

"Reach under my pillow and find your surprise, Angel." I continue to stroke myself close to orgasm. I can tell when she discovers it. A small gasp leaves her mouth as she quickly pulls it out so she can see it.

"Is this a butt plug?"

I laugh at her shock and at the term. "That is exactly what it is. Remember our discussion about sex toys? It gave me the idea of having this 'butt plug' crafted so that I can stretch your pretty asshole and make you feel so full.”

“Yes, please!” she pants. I laugh again as she squirms to see what I am doing.

“Hold still, pretty girl. I am going to come on your ass first so that we can work this in easier.”

She moans as she pops her ass closer to me. I reward her with my tongue, rimming her asshole and slowly working my tongue into the tight ring.

“Fuck,” she whispers. “You are going to make me come again if you keep doing that.”

I give her a few more licks before pulling away. “Not yet, baby. The next time you come will be when your ass is full.”

“Oh god,” she moans. Ramsey reaches back and squeezes my knot. I aim my cock so that I shoot my seed all over her perfect ass.

I grab the plug, swiping it through my cum as I work my finger into her ass. I can feel Ramsey shaking, trying to hold off her release.

“Almost, Angel.” I remove my finger and slowly begin pushing the plug into her. “Bear down and try to relax…good…almost there.”

Once I work the bulb past the tight ring of muscle, I hook my finger through the loop at the base—tugging gently. She moans at every little movement.

"You are such a good girl. So responsive. Are you ready for my cock? You are going to feel so tight, so full, Angel."

"Yes! I *need* your cock."

"Greedy girl, needing both holes filled at the same time." I slide my cock into her tight channel. She is so tight I am not sure if I will actually fit. As soon as I am almost fully in, my knot rubbing against her clit, Ramsey shatters. Fluid squirts out of her around my cock as I fuck into her.

"I can't. I can't," she says as I do not let up.

"Yes you can," I ground out. "You can take both and give me another one."

I grab the loop of the plug, working it in and out of her ass in time with my thrusts.

"You are going to give me one more, Angel. Right when I say, okay?"

She nods her agreement moaning words into the bed. I gently work the plug out of her ass, replacing it with my finger as I push my knot into her slick cunt.

"Now!" I command. Her walls clamp down on my cock as her body spasms. I come so hard I black out, collapsing on top of her. Once awareness returns, I move us on to our sides. My knot is still locked tight.

"Are you okay?" I ask as I catch my breath.

"I am so good," she replies sleepily. "Rowan is going to want one of those."

I snort. "I will have more made."

"We should design a whole collection of sex toys. Give them as gifts for birthdays and stuff."

A deep hearty laugh escapes me.

After we reluctantly pull ourselves out of bed, we get cleaned up and dressed for the day and head over to the central meeting area.

Idra gives Ramsey a knowing smirk as she hands her a tray of breakfast food. "I thought you might need to refuel," she says with a wink.

"Oh god," Ramsey replies. "I keep forgetting that there aren't any real walls around here."

"They would have heard you even if the walls were made of stone," I mumble. She hits me and I mock hurt.

"It wasn't just Ramsey that we all heard," Dex interjects as he catches up with us.

"Well, I guess there is no better time to go and discuss the many benefits of a True Mate bond," Ramsey says with a smirk.

"Maybe while we have everyone gathered, you can conduct a survey on interest in our new product ideas before they go into production," I suggest playfully.

"You know I love science." Ramsey's smile is brighter than the sun.

We sit down to eat as we wait for the others to arrive. I pick at Ramsey's plate until she swats my hand away like the queen she is. I chuckle and get up to procure my own breakfast.

Shortly after we have both finished our meals, the dining hall begins to fill up. The dispute that we are here to discuss is widely known throughout the outpost and the surrounding areas. It is uncommon for a True Mate bond to be contested, especially among family members.

The couple in question, Win and Bash, enter first, followed by their families who stand at different sides of the open space.

"Good morning," I greet.

"Good morning, Alpha," Win and Bash say in unison.

"I would like you to meet my True Mate, Ramsey," I introduce, taking her hand and pulling her closely to my side. Win and Bash both nod in respect as Ramsey offers them a cute little wave.

"I hear that you would like to seal your True Mate bond under the upcoming moon, but your parents will not consent."

"Yes, Alpha," Bash replies. "Our True Mate pairing was first discovered when my family moved to the outpost 10 years ago. Win and I were only 6 at the time."

"We have been best friends since then," Win continues. "Our feelings for each other began to, um, mature several months ago."

"We do not wish to remain apart any longer," Bash says.

I nod my understanding. Mid-teens is when our wolves typically mature. Given that Win and Bash are so close in age, it makes sense that their wolves would wish for the bond to be sealed. If there had been a larger age gap, the older would wait until the younger had reached maturity.

I call both sets of parents over. "And why is it that you do not wish for the True Mate bond to be completed?"

"I think that Bash just wants to get his cock wet. This is lust. That is all," spits Win's father.

"Your daughter is not good enough for our son. She only wants him for his talents," Bash's mother scoffs.

The bickering continues back and forth. Emotions are high but nobody brings any solid arguments to contest a True Mate pairing.

"It is true that wolves cannot lie to their True Mates, correct?" My clever Mate interrupts.

Everyone nods their agreement, the parents somewhat begrudgingly.

"Then I think that we should just ask their wolves. If they are not True Mates, the wolves would not be able to claim that they are," she suggests.

"Even if they are True Mates, my daughter is only 16. She is not mature enough to make this decision," Win's father states.

"That is an entirely different argument," I reply. "We will get to that later. But first, let's ask their wolves." I turn towards Win and Bash and speak directly into their minds, allowing Ramsey to hear the conversation as well. *"Have you found your soul within each other?"*

"Yes, Alpha," they both reply.

"Are you at the point of maturity where a True Mate bond will be appropriate?"

"Yes, Alpha," they both reply.

"I have been ready for the bond for the last year," Bash tells Win. *"You have owned my heart and soul since*

we were six years old. I cannot wait to give you my body as well."

"He has been waiting very respectfully until I was ready," Win explains. *"We told our parents about our desire to bond four moons ago. That is when they started keeping us apart. We are not able to spend time together unless we have chaperones—at least one from each family. My parents do not believe that I am ready to make this decision, but my entirety has always belonged to Bash. Even our houses being across the outpost from each other makes my wolf angry and my skin itchy."*

"We understand that feeling," Ramsey replies out loud. A few observers murmur their surprise, not expecting her to be able to hear the private mind-to-mind conversation. Technically, because she is bonded with me, she is their Alpha too. That means she should have access to communicate with anyone in the pack. But it is not something we have tried until now. "I do not have a wolf, but if I spend more than a couple of hours away from Griffin, I am unsettled. My soul pulls me to him. Hell, it pulled me from a completely different world."

"The True Mate pairing has been confirmed," I say to the crowd. "Given the nature of the next conversation, I would like to move to a private location with just Bash, Win, their parents, and my Mate."

Ramsey and I walk out of the dining hall and move in the direction of the clinic. There are not many private spaces in the outpost other than our homes. The clinic will have an open room for us to use.

Idra and Dex stand outside while Bash, Win, and their parents follow us inside.

"To be clear, we are only here because it is neutral ground. If you could learn to get along, we could have had this conversation in a more comfortable space." I am annoyed that these parents will not put the wellbeing of their children above their own drama. This conversation shouldn't even be necessary.

We enter a small clinic room that is definitely not meant to hold this many people, but we make it work. I pull Ramsey down onto my lap so that she does not need to sit next to anyone else.

"What is the age of maturity?" Ramsey asks. "I know that it is different from humans."

"Male wolves typically mature between 15 and 17. Females have a larger range. I believe it is between 14 and 18. Though, 16-18 is more common." I reply, loving the way that my Mate's beautiful brain works.

"So, clinically speaking, they are mature?"

"Yes. Their wolves would not allow them to bond if they have not yet reached maturity." I know that she knows this already. We had discussed it last night. She is doing an amazing job laying out the groundwork for our decision.

"My daughter is not ready for sex," Win's mother says, hissing the last word as if it is something that should not be said out loud.

"That is not for you to decide. It is not your right to restrict your daughter's bodily autonomy," Ramsey firmly advocates for Win.

"Then she can choose someone else!" Win's father shouts.

Ramsey flinches at his raised voice. It is subtle enough that the others do not notice, but I let out a loud growl anyway. "You will not speak to my Mate that way. Calm yourself or you will be removed from this discussion and face consequences."

"I cannot choose someone else," Win tells her father. "And, even if I could, I would still choose Bash."

"I would choose you too," Bash tells her quietly. "Even if we were not fated, I would choose you."

"I will not let my daughter stoop down to his level. She will find someone who is worthy of our line."

"That is not how True Mate bonds work," Ramsey says firmly. "It is not a choice. Win and Bash are lucky to have found each other at such a young age. They were able to grow up together, building their relationship on a foundation of friendship before adding in the physical needs that the bond creates. But this is a fated match. They cannot find another just because you want them to.”

“You will let Win and Bash seal their bond at the next full moon,” I state. “If a petty rivalry between your families is more important to you than the wellbeing of your children, you have more problems than I am able to fix today.” Turning to speak to Win and Bash directly I say, “A home will be made available to you immediately. You no longer need to live with your parents. If you choose to move to another outpost or the big village, we will find you a home there instead.” Addressing the entire group again, I state, “If their bonding does not take place due to your meddling, you will be removed from the pack for interfering with a sacred bond.”

Ramsey and I get up to leave after Win and Bash quickly give us their thanks. As we walk out the door, Ramsey stops and turns back to talk to the parents.

“I was forced to take care of my sisters when I was only 6 years old. At 8, we were removed from my parent’s care altogether because they did not prioritize our *needs* over their *wants*. Your kids want your support, but they do not need it. I suggest you sort out your priorities before you lose them.”

With that, she grabs my hand and pulls me out of the clinic. We make it only a few steps out the door before I pull her into my body and crash my lips to hers. I pour everything that I am feeling for her into this kiss. Pride, love, support, devotion—I need her to feel it all.

Several minutes later, Dex clears his throat as a not so subtle attempt to get me to stop. I can feel the audience we are attracting, but I simply couldn't care less. It is when Briar and Bree begin clapping and cheering that Ramsey ends the kiss and buries her face into my chest.

"Don't stop on our account," Briar shouts. "I just wish I would have brought snacks."

"Seeing it is almost as good as hearing it was," Bree teases as they get closer.

"Oh god!" Ramsey blushes.

"Maybe the Alpha should have positioned his lodging further from camp," Briar suggests.

"Maybe the Alpha wants everyone to hear how satisfied his Mate is," I reply.

"Anyway!" Ramsey desperately tries to change the subject. "What are you ladies up to on this fine day?"

"We were hoping that you would want to train with us a little bit. We leave tomorrow but since we will be heading closer to the border, you will be riding the Alpha the whole way," Briar explains.

"Yeah she will!" Bree says, offering me a high five.

"I will happily train with you if we can pretend like the entire outpost did not hear all of my orgasms this morning," Ramsey replies.

"I just need to find a Mate of my own so that I can have screaming orgasms for breakfast too," Briar says.

"Or, maybe you just need something to help you get there on your own," I suggest. "Ramsey told me about something that they have back in her world..." Ramsey's hand slaps over my mouth.

"Now is not the time for market research, Sweets. Why don't you go to your next meeting and I will practice being a big tough lady with Briar and Bree?"

She pushes me away, laughter filling the air as I walk towards Dex.

Chapter Eighteen

"You will be smaller and weaker than everyone who you come up against in this world." Briar has such a nice way of building me up. I am already panting, not able to get enough air into my lungs while running drills in the heat of the day.

"You need to use that to your advantage," Bree continues.

"How is being smaller and weaker an advantage?" I ask, sweat dripping from my brow. I throw myself a mini pity party before moving back into the fighting stance that they taught me.

"You can be quicker," Bree replies.

"And you can let them underestimate you. Most opponents will rely on their shifted forms—they do not even carry weapons most of the time." Briar pulls out a small dagger and thigh sheath. "They will not expect you to be armed."

I take the knife from her hands. It is lightweight and balanced. The handle fits in my hand perfectly.

"We worked with the Alpha to have this made for you. It can easily be hidden under your skirt." Bree takes it from me, ready to demonstrate some moves.

"You have mastered evasive tactics and how to get out of common holds. It is time to practice with an actual weapon." Briar pulls out an identical dagger to the one Bree is holding. They begin slowly showing me how to use them.

"I don't know if I can hurt someone," I confess. They lower their weapons and step closer to me. I have thought about it a lot. I want to be able to defend myself but if the situation arises, will I actually be able to do it? I'm not sure.

"Hopefully you will not need to. But if the choice is you or them, you must always choose yourself," Briar says firmly. Over the course of our training, I have divulged more specifics about what I have been through. What I survived. Like Dex, they began looking at me differently, but not with pity. Never with pity. They see my strength like Griffin does.

I take a deep breath. "You are right. I don't ever want to be in that position again. Okay, show me how to get stabby."

"You may be lacking the teeth and the claws, but your mind will be a stronger weapon than anything else. You have studied anatomy—so you already know the best places to strike. If your dagger is needed, you strike to kill, not to maim. Aim for large arteries. Neck. Groin. Behind the knees. You can go for a jab in the heart, but you need to be accurate and strong to get through to it. If it is a wolf that attacks, go for the neck or straight up through the jaw," Briar explains.

"You do not stop until their body stops," Bree adds. A shiver washes over me. *You do not stop until their body stops. You do not stop until they are dead—that is what they mean.* I have seen plenty of death before, working in an emergency room will expose you to that on your first shift. I have held someone's hand as they took their last breath. I have sat with families while their loved ones flatline. I have even been a part of teams who bring someone back just for their hearts to fail again. But I have never taken someone's life. Is that a mark that my soul could bear?

We continue for another hour or so before we call it a day. The sisters walk me back to the clinic, stopping first to grab some lunch, before they leave to spend the rest of the day with their parents.

Griffin is at the clinic when I walk in. We chat for a little while about the training that I just did and then the expectant mother arrives.

The healer makes introductions before we all head back into a private exam room. "Linnea is due with a single pup within the next week. I was hoping that you might be able to check and see if there are any potential complications that are already making themselves known," she explains to me.

Griffin stiffens beside me. I'm not sure either of us really understood why I was requested for this appointment.

"I can try." I have never used my magic proactively before, but if there is an abnormality present, I don't see why I wouldn't be able to find it. "Are you okay with me using my magic to look internally? I will need to touch your belly, but you shouldn't feel anything else."

Linnea looks a little hesitant but nods her consent.

"I will talk through what I am doing during your exam. If you feel anything unusual or want me to stop, just say so. If for some reason I cannot hear you, Griffin will get my attention."

"Okay," Linnea says. I can tell that she is still feeling nervous. I channel my calm as I try to reassure her with my eyes that it will all be okay. Internally, I am freaking out a bit. I am not sure if this is something that I can even do. And I am feeling the heat of being put on the spot.

I place my hand on Linnea's stomach and close my eyes. I picture in my mind what everything is supposed to look like before pushing my magic through my hand and into her body.

I can hear her gasp as my magic takes hold.

"Does everything feel okay, Linnea?" I ask quietly.

"Yes. Sorry. I was just surprised by the glowing," she replies.

I nod. "I apologize. I forgot to mention that part. My sister calls me a glow worm."

I can hear her chuckle, which puts us all at ease again.

"I am going to have a little look around now, okay? You shouldn't feel anything," I remind her.

With my magic, I take a look inside her belly. Her fluid levels and walls all look like they should. When I turn my attention to her baby, I notice that the umbilical cord is looped loosely around the baby's neck. It is something that could work itself out as the baby moves around, but I don't want to take any chances if it is something that I can fix.

"Linnea, I do not see any tears or weak spots that may lead to heavy bleeding. However, the umbilical cord is wrapped loosely around your baby's neck. I am going to try to unwrap it. It should not hurt but you might feel some movement."

"Okay," she replies. "Is my baby okay?"

"Yes. They are wiggling around. Everything else looks good," I reply.

I focus on what it is supposed to look like and use my magic to untwist the cord. Once I am happy with how everything looks, I pull my magic back and open my eyes.

"It worked. I think that you should probably deliver within the next couple of days. The baby looks fully developed. Would you like to know the gender?"

"You were able to tell?" Her words are a mix of shock and excitement.

"Yes," I chuckle.

"Can my Mate come in before you tell me?"

"Of course," I reply.

Griffin sends a message out to her Mate requesting that he join us. Linnea explained that he would normally have been here for the appointment, but he has a custom tapestry that he needs to finish and deliver before their baby is born.

A few minutes later, he rushes in.

"Everything is okay, honey," she tells him. "The Alpha's Mate has special magic. She is able to tell us the gender of our baby. Do you want to know?"

He lets out a relieved breath. "I want to know if you do," he tells her, planting a kiss on her forehead.

Linnea looks over at me and nods. "We would love to find out. Maybe we will be able to finally agree on a name."

"You are having a beautiful baby girl. She already has a full head of hair and was sucking her thumb." I let out a little laugh.

"A baby girl?" Linnea says with happy tears in her eyes. Her Mate pulls her into a hug.

"Congratulations," Griffin says.

We excuse ourselves, leaving the happy family alone to celebrate.

"You amaze me every single day," Griffin tells me.

"I really didn't know if I could do it. I have only mended before. I wasn't sure if my magic would be able to unwrap the cord."

"How did you do it?"

"I just pictured what I wanted to do and my magic made it happen." I shrug. I need to find a way to practice with my magic more so that I can find my limits. Maybe Griffin will be able to help me think of a way without needing to use people when we get back to the lodge.

"I am so proud of you, Angel."

Our lips connect in a sweet, lazy kiss. Griffin is the only person other than my sisters, who has ever felt proud of me. I don't know how I got so lucky to find a partner that is unconditionally supportive.

"What do you think about having dinner in bed?" he asks against my lips.

"Are you on the menu?"

He chuckles, moving his lips down to my neck. "Real food first. We can have each other for dessert."

We are about to enter our lodging when a flurry of activity catches our attention towards the other side of the outpost, near the clinic that we just came from.

Griffin grabs my hand, and we run towards the chaos. As we get closer, I can see that there is a large man holding a small child, pleading with the healer to help. We don't stop running until we are standing at the healer's side.

"What happened?" Griffin asks.

"My son," the man says in panicked breaths. "We were out foraging, and my son came in contact with Nightshade. I didn't see it until it was too late. He ingested it."

Nightshade. Belladonna. It can cause hallucinations, rashes, vomiting, and in some cases, death. But that is for humans. I do not know if it affects wolf shifters differently.

"We have this in my world too. But how does it affect shifters? I haven't read any chapters on what is poisonous here yet," I ask Griffin. I do not want to worry the father further if I can help it.

"Death," he tells me ominously.

I nod my head, knowing what I must do.

"I have Moon Blessed magic," I tell the father, not wanting to waste any time. "I think I can help." Turning to the healer, I ask, "What would you normally do for Nightshade poisoning?"

"Nothing," she says. "There is nothing that can be done. It is too toxic."

"Let me try?" I ask the father. He agrees instantly, desperate for his son to get better.

Walking closer, I push past my anxiety and place my hand on the boy's abdomen.

"Careful," Griffin warns quietly behind me. "Even touching it can be deadly. If he has it on his body..."

"I will be okay," I reassure him. "When my magic activates, my body glows like moonlight," I tell the father.

We have amassed a crowd, everyone curious about if I will actually be able to help this little boy. I block them all out and push my magic into the boy's body as he mutters incoherently and shakes. I have never done anything like this before. I'm not even sure if I can. But I know that he needs to vomit up the poison. Back in New York, we would have administered activated charcoal and given supportive medications to rid the body of the poison and alleviate some of the symptoms. That is not an option right now, so I will just need to use my magic instead. Focusing my magic on the child's diaphragm and lower stomach, I activate the nerve impulses that send signals to the brain and cause vomiting.

His body begins to heave, and I can feel Griffin stepping around me to help the father support his son, but I keep my magic within his body, not pulling back until he is clear of the poison.

Not used to using my magic as much as I did today, I nearly collapsed into Griffin's arms, shaking and sweating, but incredibly grateful that I was able to save this little boy's life.

I do not remember walking back to our lodging. I don't remember Griffin washing my body, feeding me, or tucking me into bed. But I know that it happened. And when exhaustion overwhelms me, I welcome the dark. Because with Griffin, my needs are met. I am safe. And he will always be there to catch me.

Chapter Nineteen

Ramsey

The next morning, we wake early, wanting to arrive at our final outpost before the sun sets. Both the panther territory and a portion of Nightfury territory lie within a few miles of the outpost that we are visiting. Because Dreena and her followers crossed through this outpost on their way out of Nighthowl, Griffin wants us all to be extra cautious.

From what I was told, the panther shifters mostly keep to themselves but can be unpredictable when provoked.

Briar told me that Nightfury has an outpost less than a day's journey from where we will be.

We move quickly through the territory. Griffin sets a hard pace, but Dex and our guards do not have trouble keeping up. If I was running, I would have been left in the dust. It is extremely hot today—it must be over 100 degrees—so I don't mind spending the time seated comfortably on Griffin's back with the wind in my hair.

Stopping along the bank of a river for lunch, I walk out into the water to cool myself down. The river is so clear and refreshing, I lift my skirt and wade in a little deeper.

Two dark wolves jump in after me and wrestle each other in the water. Giggling, I splash them to join in on the fun. Two strong arms wrap around me as I am pulled into a strong, naked body.

"I think you are a bad influence," Griffin whispers in my ear. "Our guards are having way too much fun."

"Oh, let them be." I twist around in his arms. "Briar and Bree deserve to have a little fun every now and then."

Griffin seals his lips to mine and I lose myself in him for a little while. Before we know it, Dex is calling us back in so that we can move on.

Griffin shifts and scoops me up right in the water. I squeal as water splashes all around me.

"I love making you wet," he says into my mind.

"I'm sure you do, naughty boy," I laugh.

The rest of our day is spent weaving between trees. The hot sun beats down on us, but the leaves offer us some shade. The light shining through the varied greens of the leaves looks like stained glass. It is beautiful.

It isn't long before I can see the outpost up ahead. This is the smallest outpost that we have stayed at. It makes us all a little more cautious, but Griffin has received word about a string of thefts happening and he needs to sort it out before we make our journey back to the lodge.

We are greeted by the families that reside at the outpost—four families and two single wolves. They all seem close and friendly. Between the four families, there are two young children, one pregnant mother, and a newly Mated pair. One of the single wolves is an elderly woman—she looks like she is around the same age as Heka, though it is kind of hard to tell based on how wolves age. The other single wolf is a young man who looks to be younger than Griffin—which could be anywhere from 20 to 100 years old.

Other than the yurt that is always available for Griffin to use, tents have been set up to house our traveling party around a fire pit. Griffin explained to me that this outpost does not have many visitors due to its location, so extra semi-permanent housing is not needed.

One of the males approaches us as we get our group sorted. This guy is huge, almost as big as Griffin. I flinch when he gets a little too close. Griffin shifts and protectively pulls me behind him. The male bows his head in respect for his Alpha but looks at me curiously.

"It is good to see you, Alpha," he says.

"It has been a while." Griffin moves me to his side, keeping his arm around me. "Jovan, this is my True Mate, Ramsey. Ramsey, this is Jovan. He used to be with Bade's pack but transferred when he met his Mate, Indi." Griffin indicates Jovan's Mate, the pregnant woman I noticed as we entered.

"It is nice to meet you," I say. "And congratulations."

"Thank you, Alpha," Jovan replies.

"Please call me Ramsey," I say out of habit. Curiosity flashes in his eyes, but to his credit, he does not look to Griffin for approval before nodding, like many others have done.

"I hear you have been dealing with some thefts over the last few weeks. What has been stolen?" Griffin wastes no time getting straight to business.

"Mostly food stores, some tools, furs, and weapons." Jovan quickly looks around, "I have looked throughout the camp and they are not here. I do not believe the thief is one of us," he adds quietly.

Griffin nods, also looking around at the group.

"Any sign of Dreena or her followers?" Griffin asks Jovan privately, allowing me to listen in.

"They passed through about three weeks ago. Cleared us out of food but left us alone otherwise. I kept everyone here mostly out of sight. They stayed in their homes, allowing me to be the only contact. When they realized who I was, they took our food and left."

"Good work. Are you able to make due with the supplies that you still have?"

"The nearest Nightfury outpost is going to send us some more tools and weapons. We have been able to hunt enough to start refilling our food stores."

"Good. Let me know if you need any assistance and I will have some supplies sent here," Griffin says.

"When is your Mate due?" I ask as Griffin calls Indi over.

"Any day now," Jovan replies, wrapping an arm around her. "We do not have a healer here, but Xylia has delivered many pups in her years."

"Would you mind having an appointment with me? I am a nurse."

"I would love that," Indi replies. "We are pretty sure that I am carrying twins," she adds quietly.

I offer her a smile, hopefully relieving some of the worry that she must be feeling.

"Tomorrow morning we can find some privacy and I will take a look and listen."

After making sure that our group is settled, we grab some dinner and make our way to our lodgings.

"Do you think it is Dreena and her followers who have been stealing?" I ask as we lay in bed.

"I do not know," he answers. "It could be them. They would have the need for tools and weapons. We know that they did not take any as they passed through the other outposts, but being closer to where they wanted to set up camp, it is possible that they came back for supplies. Based on what Bade said, though, it is still a two-day run from here to where they settled."

"Who else could it be?" I wonder.

"The panthers are the only other real threat in this area—unless it is a lone wolf moving through."

"Why would the panthers steal from here? I thought they would only attack if provoked." Briar told me that the panthers are incredibly secretive. They keep to themselves because they do not want anyone poking around.

"Typically, yes. But we do not know if they were provoked by anyone. With Dreena and her followers stirring everything up, it is possible that the effects were felt in the other territories. We do not have much contact with them, but some of my wolves trade that way. War has also noticed our food sources shifting their patterns. One change here could ripple to them."

A butterfly effect. "Well, hopefully we can find who it is. It seems like Jovan is able to keep this outpost protected, at least."

"Yeah. He was one of Bade's best soldiers. He has good instincts and is a strong fighter. Honestly, he could probably beat me in a match—though he would never try." Griffin chuckles.

"Hopefully it will not come to fighting." I listen to the steady beat of Griffin's heartbeat under my ear as I drift off to sleep.

Chapter Twenty

Griffin gently shakes me awake a few hours later. "Angel, Indi is in labor. We must get up."

I sit up and immediately start feeling for my clothes in the dark. After getting dressed, I quickly tie my hair back in a braid as we head out the door. I can hear Indi's cries from across the small outpost.

Running through the camp, I mentally flip through pictures of what healthy twin gestation looks like for wolf-shifters. It is similar to that of humans, though the outer wall needs to be thicker for the wolves. I remind myself that the babies might be shifted. That was definitely a shock the first time I saw it.

I enter Indi and Jovan's home without knocking. Griffin is hot on my heels. Their home is similar to Griffin's lodging here. Everything is in one larger circular room. I find Indi on her hands and knees on the bed while Jovan rubs her lower back. She is completely bare with fluids leaking down her thighs. I can smell the metallic tinge of blood and as I get closer, I can see that the fluid is pink.

"Hi, Indi. I am going to help you have these babies, okay?" She nods as she breathes through another contraction.

"Indi, is it okay if I check to see how dilated you are?"

"Yes. I do not think that I can move from this position though," she replies.

"That is okay. You can stay in whichever position feels best for you. Jovan keep rubbing her back and reminding her to breathe. Griffin, can you find some fresh water and towels?"

I crouch down behind Indi, reaching up to see how quickly this labor is progressing.

"You are doing so well, Indi. You are already close to being fully dilated. You do have some bleeding, so I would like to find the cause of that. I have Moon Touched magic that can allow me to look inside and heal. Is it okay if I use my magic to help you? You should not feel a thing."

"Yes," she nods.

"Please do whatever you can to help them," Jovan says.

"I will," I promise. "I do start to glow when my magic is being used. Please do not be frightened."

Coming up to stand next to me with fresh water and towels, Griffin gives my shoulder an encouraging squeeze.

I press my hand to Indi's belly, pushing my magic out in search of the source of the bleeding. I find a small tear towards the top of her uterus and mend the wound. I then take a quick look at the babies.

"Indi, you had a small tear that I mended. Everything else looks okay except the first baby in line to make their entrance into the world is lined up to come out butt first. That is not ideal for either of you, so I am going to try to rotate them into the proper position, okay?"

"Okay," she replies through gritted teeth. She is having some pretty intense contractions.

"Have you ever done this before?" I hear Jovan ask.

"She has not done this specifically, but she did unwrap an umbilical cord and has aided in a successful twin birth in addition to assisting hundreds of non-magical births back in her world," Griffin explains. "Your Mate is in very capable hands."

Sweat is dripping down my back and forehead as I concentrate on slowly moving the baby. I hear a crash outside and almost lose my focus.

"What was that?" Griffin asks Jovan.

"We set up a trap in our supply shed hoping to catch the thief."

"I will have Dex check it out."

"You might feel some pressure as I move the baby, Indi. If it hurts, let me know and I will stop and we will try something else," I explain.

"Dex said that the trap caught a female panther shifter. She masked her scent and was nearly impossible to see in the dark if it hadn't been for the trap blocking her escape," Griffin quietly tells Jovan.

"I am almost there, Indi. How are you feeling?"

"The contractions feel worse," she pants.

"You are doing such a good job," I tell her. "Jovan, help your Mate breathe through the contractions."

Once I have the baby positioned correctly, I make sure that the other baby will follow nicely before pulling my magic back. That procedure took more effort than anything that I have done before and I feel like I am seconds from passing out.

I feel my legs start to give out as Griffin catches me.

"Are you okay, Angel?"

"I think so. I just feel a bit woozy."

"You used too much power. You need to rest."

"Not until the babies are born. I just need to sit for a minute."

I can see the worry etched upon his face. He knows that there isn't anything that will stop me from helping this mother, though. She needs me more than I need to rest. Especially since this is a twin birth and anything could happen.

"I promise that I am fine," I reassure him.

Just then, the camp turns into pure chaos around us. We can hear yelling and growling. It sounds like buildings are being destroyed.

"Fuck! We are under attack," Griffin shouts. "It is Dreena's supporters. They found out that we are here."

"Go," I tell him. He looks at me like I have lost my mind. "They need you out there more than I need you in here. I will be fine. Jovan, they will need you too."

"I am not leaving my Mate," Jovan growls at me.

Mustering up as much strength as I can, I stand my ground. "We are in much more danger if they make their way in here. You need to stop them before they get all of the way through camp."

"You will tell me if you need help," Griffin tells me—it is not a question. "Are you armed?"

I flash him my thigh. "I can protect us if I need to. But I need you to go and stop them before they get in here."

Griffin gives me a hard kiss while Jovan does the same to Indi. "Protect my family," he says as he heads towards the door with Griffin.

I hear Indi let out a quiet sob, which has me rushing to her side.

"I am going to help you have these babies. It will all be okay." I hope that I am giving her a little more confidence than I am feeling right now.

Chapter Twenty-One

Griffin

I leave Ramsey and join the fight outside. So far, the actual fighting has been kept to a minimum. It is mostly just Dreena's followers yelling hateful garbage while Dex and our five guards position themselves in a defensive formation. The other men in the camp are standing protectively in front of their families. Well—other than the single male, Reyes. He is standing in front of the supply shed. Maybe he is standing guard over the thief?

I signal to Dex in question.

"Reyes is insisting that the panther is his Mate. He will not leave her unguarded." Bloody Mother. What in the fuck is going on tonight?

"Indi is in labor. Ramsey is aiding her. We need to draw attention away."

Dex nods his understanding as I send the same message out to our guards.

Dreena's lackeys are still spewing hate. Apparently, they were notified of our arrival to this outpost and if we hand over 'the witch' they will not kill us. Normally, I would laugh, but they do have a lot of support with them. We are severely outnumbered.

I walk out to the front. They already know that I am here so there is no point in trying to sneak up on them. "Enough!" I command. I direct my Alpha dominance at the enemy. Everyone is affected, some shaking where they stand while others shift into their wolves. I may be the mildest Alpha out of the three of us, but I am still an Alpha. The tell-tale scent of urine fills the air. Good. They should be scared. "You dare come into my territory to attack my Mate?" I growl.

"Your Mate is a witch!"

"You are under her spell!"

"She will be the end of the packs!"

It is all lies that we have heard before.

"I am really getting tired of this hateful propaganda. My Mate is not a witch. She is my True Mate, and we are Moon Touched." I lift my hands up, not in surrender, but to display the silver moon markings covering my skin. "The magic that she has is a result of our bonding and our blessing. Your leader has filled your head with lies. She was upset that my brother refused her pathetic attempts to bring him to bed." I cannot believe how Dreena's lies have turned so many against us. "She has used fear to manipulate you."

I glance around the camp, noting the damage that was done to the structures. "What was your goal here? What did you think would happen?" I ask.

"Hand her over and we will walk away," one of the idiots suggests, ignoring my question.

"I am Alpha." I bark. "You do not get to make demands of me or my Mate."

"We have families too. Mates. The witch is a threat to our families," one of the males states.

"If that were the case, you would know that there is nothing that I wouldn't do to protect my Mate. There is nothing that Jovan wouldn't do to protect his Mate. There is nothing that Reyes wouldn't do to protect his Mate. You may have more in numbers, but that just means more of you will have to die. You are on the wrong side of this fight."

"It is your Mate who must die," one of them spits out.

"Anyone who tries to attack my Mate will die. Your actions will determine how brutally. I do not give a flying fuck if you are from Nighthowl, Nightfang, or Nightfury. I am Alpha. A threat to my Mate makes me your judge, juror, and executioner," I growl with dominance.

"Dreena is our Alpha," more than one of the wolves sneers.

I laugh. "Dreena is not an Alpha. From what War told me, there is actually nothing remarkable about her. He turned down her advances for years. She is just a pathetic female who did not like being told 'no'." I know that I am goading them. But, I need to stall for time while we come up with a plan. "Where is Dreena, anyway? Is she too afraid to show herself? Or were you all gullible enough to be sent on a suicide mission?"

"Dreena cares about the Pack."

"How did she get you to believe her lies? Did she fuck all of you? Tell you that she would become the next Alpha and choose one of you to share in her power? You do remember that she cannot simply declare herself Alpha, right? There must be a peaceful transition of power between the current Alphas and next. After that was done, the new Alpha would need to be strong enough to withstand holding the bonds of the Pack within themselves. Dreena is not capable of doing that. You have backed the wrong wolf. You fell for her sugary words and promises without considering basic knowledge of your own species."

Their growls intensify. I seem to have struck a chord. I slowly walk, repositioning focus away from the homes behind me.

"I guarantee that she sees you all as disposable. It is why you are here facing an Alpha, and she is nowhere in sight."

Our guards are closing in as we slowly shift everyone away from our women and children.

Ramsey's scream cuts through the night and all hell breaks loose. Dreena's followers shift into their wolves and lunge at us. We are stronger, but they have us beat in numbers. We need to focus and make sure nobody sneaks through our lines.

"Angel, are you okay?" I shout through our bond as I fight off three attackers at once. Tearing through their necks, I am met with more. *"Ramsey! I need to hear that you are okay,"* I try again to get through to her. I can feel through the bond that she is alive, but it worries me that she cannot communicate. Did she pass out? Were they attacked? Why did she scream?

I look around as we fight off our assailants. We are all taking on multiple attackers at the same time.

Dreena's followers appear to be more organized than we originally thought. Another wave of wolves appears from across the valley. I am about to end another life when they shift and start laughing.

"By the time you find her, you will be too late. Dreena will have her revenge on the witches. She will kill them all!"

I slice through his throat, blood spurting up and hitting me in the face. I look over to see that Jovan is locked in battle with several wolves. He will not be able to get to Ramsey any easier than I can. I am surrounded on all sides by attackers, but I need to get to her.

"Ramsey! Dreena is here. Protect yourself until I can get to you!"

I do not know if she is hearing me and is unable to respond or if she has already been attacked. The threat to my Mate transforms me into a beast. I tear through everyone in my path. When I make it back to Jovan's home, I have left a trail of bodies in my wake. I will not leave any of Dreena's followers alive tonight.

"There are too many of them," Dex calls out to me.

"Reyes, will your Mate help us?" It is a bit of a wildcard move, but panthers are fierce fighters.

"She does not even know that she is my Mate. They would not let me talk to her," he growls.

216

"Tell her. Ask her to help. If she agrees, you can release her. We need her help."

I burst through Jovan's door to find Ramsey holding her dagger, covered in blood, standing over a crumpled body.

Chapter Twenty-Two

Griffin and Jovan have just left. I am holding Indi's hand as she continues to breathe through contractions. She is fully dilated and her babies are coming soon.

"I need to wait," she tells me. "I cannot have them right now. I need to keep them safe in my belly."

"I know, sweetie," I tell her calmly. I still feel wiped out after using too much magic. I am unsteady on my feet, so I sit in the bed with my patient. "We can wait just a little while to see if things get sorted out quickly. But these babies are coming tonight. They are ready to meet you."

"How can I bring them into the world in the middle of a battle?"

"We will just take everything one step at a time, okay?" We are speaking softly. I am doing everything that I can to keep Indi calm while I am internally freaking the fuck out. What do I do if they find us? My fingers brush against the cool metal strapped to my thighs. I help save lives. I don't know if I could actually end one. With the awful sounds of battle being the only thing that I can hear over the blood rushing in my ears, I know that I will do anything that I need to do to protect my patient and her babies.

"Keep breathing, Indi. I know that it hurts but breathing will help."

I tried to get an update from Griffin, but I think that my power is too drained. I can sense him, but I do not have the energy to follow the connection like I normally do. The magic is still there, but it is so low that using whatever I have left would cause burnout. I will not be a help to anyone if I pass out.

"Tell me about your world," Indi says. I appreciate the distraction. I think that she realized that we both needed one.

"The world that I came from had no magic. We had technology that allowed us to do things we wouldn't normally be able to do, like talk to someone from a long distance, or travel quickly, but it was really just humans and machines. The city that I lived in with my sisters was called New York City. It was huge. Over 8 million people lived in the city alone. We were not split up by packs but there were different neighborhoods within the city. My sisters and I lived in a small apartment in Queens." I continue rambling about our life there. My job as a nurse, Rowan and Reese and everything that we did together to have fun. I distract her through several more contractions before I see movement near the door. I keep talking as I reposition my body to stand between the door and Indi.

A female wolf slinks in. At first, I think that it might be Ebony—the coloring and size are the same—but her eyes are all wrong. They show nothing but hate. I scream as she lunges, snapping her maw like a rabid beast, taunting me before she stalks back towards the outer edge of the room. She does it again as she chuffs and snarls. She is playing with me, feeding off of my fear.

"Ramsey! Dreena is here. Protect yourself until I can get to you!" Griffin's warning rings in my head right as she snaps again, remaining much closer than before.

Maybe if I stall, Griffin or Jovan will get back here in time. I take a breath and remove all signs of fright from my face. I cannot stop my shaking hands, but I can control my mouth, my voice. "Shift so I can speak to you," I command. I am only an Alpha in title but I do my best to channel the Alpha energy that I know my Mate is capable of. Hoping, praying, that some of his dominance transferred over to me when we bonded. The wolf whimpers and then shakes her head and snarls at me. "Shift!" I command again.

The wolf in front of me shifts into a woman. She is beautiful. Tall. Her deeply tanned skin and pitch-black hair make a striking combination. But her eyes are wild. Not the mischievous wild that sometimes takes over Griffin's beautiful blues. The wild in her eyes is almost black, unhinged. She looks at me with pure hate and growls as she takes in the scene behind me. I have never met her before, but I know that this must be Dreena.

"Hello, witch," she sneers at me. "Using your black magic to infect more innocent wolves, are you?" Her eyes keep shifting as she cackles at me. I take a closer look at her. Despite her beauty, there are cracks in her facade; little openings that paint a more accurate depiction of her true self. Red lines mar her skin as if she cannot help but scratch an imaginary itch. That they are not healed tells me that it is a frequent issue. Like something is trying to crawl itself out of her skin. "Caught in the act. Naughty witch. Infecting wolves before they are even born? Three witches so far, soon to be no more."

If she had come in as a patient back in New York, I would think that she is in the middle of a psychiatric episode. Trying to remember my training from when I did a rotation with the psych ward, I keep calm. Assess for danger to herself or anyone else, including me. The fact that she can turn into a literal predator with claws and teeth is a pretty big threat. Her broken mind is another one. I need to do whatever I can to prevent danger to the laboring mother behind me, her unborn babies, and myself.

"I am not a witch. I am a nurse," I explain, my voice steady. "I am helping a mother in need. Please leave us so that I can help my patient."

Her voice singsongs as she speaks again. "One witch traps; her magic used to steal the Alpha. He was mine before she came along. He did not know but will never forget. I was what he needed but she whispered her spell and he was trapped. Stuck with the temptress until I rescue him. Two witches use magic to pull mates apart. They meddle, those witches. She was sick but meddled anyway, casting her spell. She is weak, like one witch. Too weak. Not a threat for long. Three witches use stolen magic to infect us. Infect and steal, steal and infect. But infect no longer."

Her words come out in a jumbled nonsensical mess. Like a twisted-up nursery rhyme. She paces back and forth, licking her chapped lips and clawing her nails over her face—scratching so deep that blood begins to bead on her cheeks.

"I am a nurse. I help people who are hurt. Do you need help, Dreena? Have you been hurt?"

Indi yells out in pain. Her contractions are too close and strong. The babies are coming now.

Dreena's crazed eyes dart behind me, snaring Indi in her sight. "Infected! She is infected but she yells in pain. Her body rejects you just like I do."

"She is not infected, Dreena. She is in labor. Her babies are ready to be brought into this world. I need to help her. Please let me help her. I will not use any magic. I am just a nurse." It was a last-ditch effort, appealing to any scraps of compassion that might still exist somewhere within her.

Unfortunately, it is not enough.

It happens so quickly, I do not even have time to think. Dreena shifts and lunges for me, aiming for my throat. I rip the dagger out of the sheath on my thigh and slice through her neck—just like we practiced. Dreena did not expect me to be armed, and I sliced clean through her jugular. It was messy but quick. Effective, despite my shaking hand. Her form crumpled to the ground right as the door opened again. Griffin shifts from his wolf at the sight of me standing over Dreena's still body, staring at her to make sure that she stops.

You are smaller and weaker. Faster. Use your knowledge. Strike to kill. You do not stop until their body stops. You do not stop until their body stops. You do not stop until their body stops.

Griffin approaches slowly, as if I might spook. Maybe I will. I have never killed a person before. *Strike to kill. You do not stop until their body stops.*

I am still standing over her body.

She isn't moving.

She has stopped.

A hand reaches out and I flinch. Then I see him. He has pulled me from Hell in my dreams. He will help me here too. It is Griffin. He is safe. He loves me. His blue eyes swirl with worry; but also pride and love.

I let him help me.

I don't realize that my entire body is shaking until Griffin gently takes the bloody dagger from my hand. I try to keep it, desperately gripping it in my hand. I need it, just in case. But he takes it from my shaking hand anyway. "You have another," he reminds me softly. I reach down and feel for the blade attached to my other thigh. *I have another.* I can still protect myself.

"You are safe, Angel. You are safe." He repeats that over and over as he pulls me into his arms.

"Did I... Is she... I..."

"You protected yourself and Indi."

I protected myself and Indi. I repeated his words in my head.

Indi.

Indi!

I snap out of whatever trance I have been in and spin around to move closer to Indi. Indi who must be scared out of her mind right now. Indi who just watched me kill someone while she is trying to keep her babies from being born in the middle of a blood bath.

"Are you okay?" I ask her hesitantly. What else do you say in this situation?

She takes my bloody hand in hers, holding it tightly to her chest. "You protected me and my babies. Thank you."

I try to hold it together, but a sob breaks through. Griffin stands behind me, holding my still shaking body close to his.

"I let our group know that Dreena is gone. The battle is over," Griffin says quietly.

Jovan busts through the door and runs to Indi's side. He has a few bloody wounds but nothing life threatening. After checking Indi over, he looks around his home and takes in the full picture of what happened. I think he is about to say something when Indi cries out again in pain. The sound jolts me out of my inner spiral again and I focus my energy back on my patient.

"Those babies are ready to come out now. They have been waiting so patiently for us, haven't they, Indi?"

"Yes. But they are not being patient any longer. Honey," she turns to Jovan, "can you help the Alpha remove the body?" She says it in a whisper, probably for my benefit. I think everyone in this room can tell that I am holding myself together by a thread.

"I'm going to be honest with you, Indi, I do not have any control over my magic at the moment, so we are going to have to do this the old-fashioned way. Luckily, I actually have more experience doing this without magic anyway. At your next contraction, you are going to bear down and push. Are you okay with Griffin being in here? I can ask him to wait outside if it would make you feel more comfortable, but he is not going to want to leave me right now."

"He can stay. You need someone to support you, too," she says as she gives my hand a squeeze, tears fall freely from my eyes as I muster up any last dregs of strength that I have.

"Alright boys, make yourselves useful. Grab a leg and help support her."

I wash my hands, trying hard not to look at the blood as it washes into the basin, and then head back over to the bed where Indi is now flanked by two very large, and very naked men. I rummage around in their cupboard and pull out two pairs of pants. I know that nudity is not a big thing for shifters, but I need to have a little normalcy for my own sake right now.

Griffin calls for Xylia, the older female from the outpost, who comes in right as the first baby is being born. She doesn't hesitate to scoop him up with a clean cloth, clearing his airways and rubbing on him until he lets out a loud wail. We all let out a breath of relief as we wait on the next baby. About 10 minutes later, the second twin is born. Another boy who looks identical to the first. His cries immediately join his brother's as I pass him over to Jovan. Both babies are snuggled up against Indi's chest as I finish cleaning up.

I am about to excuse myself when my legs give out and I collapse into a heap on the floor. Griffin rushes over and pulls me into his arms.

"You did such a good job, Angel," he tells me quietly.

My body has started to shake again. My mouth is dry and my breathing is all wrong. I am starting to crash from adrenaline and shock.

"Deep breaths, love." I try to follow Griffin as he leads me through a breathing exercise. "You were so brave. So strong." Griffin stands with me in his arms, carrying me out the door and through the outpost to our lodging. He has my head tucked close to his neck and is covering my eyes with his hand. He doesn't want me to see what I am sure is a gruesome sight. Even with my face pressed into his body, I almost vomit at the potent copper scent of blood in the air.

There is warm water waiting for us as we enter our home for the night. Griffin fills the bathtub and gently lowers me into the water. My shaking becomes worse as I feel his body step away from mine.

"I am just grabbing some soap and a cloth, Angel. I will be right there."

He returns almost immediately, lowering himself into the water behind me. Griffin slowly washes our bodies and hair. The water is bloody so I look up at the ceiling. Once we are clean, Griffin pulls me out of the tub and dries us off. We crawl into bed and he holds me as I cry.

It must be early morning by the time my tears dry and I drift off to sleep. When I wake, the sun is already high in the sky. We were supposed to head home today. I am not sure if I can even pull myself out of bed, though I know I have to. Griffin pulls me tighter to his chest when I start to move.

"Stay," he says quietly.

"What time is it? Did you sleep at all?"

"It is around lunch time," he tells me. "I got some sleep while you did. Are you okay?"

I nod as tears well up in my eyes.

He wipes them from my cheek when they start to fall.

"Logically," I tell him, "I know that I did what I had to do. She was acting like she was in the middle of a psychotic break. When she lunged for my throat, I didn't even think. I grabbed the dagger and sliced. She was going to kill me and then kill Indi because she thought that I had infected her and her babies with my magic. I had to do it."

"You did the right thing, sweetheart."

"But I ended her life. I did that." My voice cracks as I tell him.

"You defended yourself and Indi. You saved lives."

"And I would do it again," I confess quietly. "I think that is the hardest pill to swallow. I would do it again if it meant saving Indi. I would do it again if it came down to me or her because I know that I am meant to be here—to help—to save lives. I would do it again if it means protecting my sisters from her hate. I would do it again."

Griffin tilts my chin and places a gentle kiss on my lips. "You would do it again because you are strong," he tells me. "You would do it again because you needed to protect innocent lives. You would do it again because you are absolutely meant to be here, to help others, and to live a full life. You showed incredible strength and bravery last night in more ways than just your interaction with Dreena. You were strong and brave for Indi. You used incredible magic to heal and save innocent lives before they even entered the world. You are amazing, Angel." Griffin reassures me with his lips and pours all of his love for me into his kiss. After a little while, I am feeling a bit more steady.

I am not sure if I can handle the answer, but I need to ask anyway. "Were there any other casualties?"

"Not from the outpost. Jovan has trained all of the wolves at this outpost to fight, to protect themselves. Even the pups," he replies. "There were not any survivors from the group that attacked," he adds hesitantly.

"Why did they attack us here?" I know that Dreena was leading the charge for this witch hunt, but we didn't see any of her supporters while we were traveling through Nighthowl.

"Someone had tipped them off that we were here. I do not know for sure, but I am guessing it was someone from the last outpost. There were so many that witnessed your magic there," he explains. "They came for you. Everyone from our group and those that live here all fought and defended bravely. We were severely outnumbered, but we were stronger. Plus, we had a panther working with us at the end."

"What?! The panther from the storage shed? How did that happen?"

"Apparently the thief was a young panther female. She felt the pull to her Mate but did not realize that was what was making her come back here. She stole food and weapons to supply her den."

"Her Mate?"

"Yeah. The young wolf who recently moved here, Reyes. He felt the pull too but did not realize what it was until she was captured in the trap that Jovan had set. During the fight, Reyes would not leave her unprotected so I asked him if he could talk to her about fighting with us. Panthers are vicious when they feel their Mates or cubs are in danger. Once she recognized Reyes as her Mate, she joined the fight in protecting the outpost."

I can't help my chuckle at how that all unfolded.

"It is so good to hear that sound again," he tells me as he pulls me impossibly closer. "I was so afraid last night when I could not contact you."

"I think I used too much power. I felt so drained. I could feel you but I couldn't follow our line of communication until your warning came through. It helped me figure out what was happening."

"I am just so thankful that you are okay. I came for you as soon as I could."

"I love you," I tuck my face against his neck.

"I love you, too, Angel," he says with a kiss to my head.

Chapter Twenty-Three

Griffin

Light filters in through a slit in the door. Luckily, the damage done to the outpost was mostly contained to the common areas. All housing had survived with little repairs needed. Even Jovan and Indi's home only needed cleaning. More importantly, injuries were minor, and no lives were taken, other than Dreena and her army that ambushed us. They are all dead.

I normally would have helped with the clean-up, but Ramsey needed me more. I could not bear to separate myself from her—even if all I could do was hold her while she slept. Everyone understood that. What she experienced, taking a life for the first time, is not something that you will ever forget. The number of lives that I ended yesterday is more than I ever have in my 107 years. It was a complete slaughter. But I would do it again. Maybe that leaves a mark on my soul, but I cannot feel an ounce of regret for doing what needed to be done to protect my Mate. Even if I did not arrive in time to save her from the terror and guilt that plagued her.

After she cried, depleting her body of all its tears, she fell into a fitful sleep, haunted by memories—old and new. She thrashed and screamed but did not wake. I ran clean washcloths over her body, not knowing what else to do but remembering that baths have helped her in the past. Her body, made stronger by her training, felt so fragile as it shook and trembled.

We have not left our lodging all day. Ramsey woke briefly before letting sleep take her again. In addition to the emotional strain of the night before, she almost completely depleted her magic. Her body will force her to rest until she is able to refill that well.

Deciding that I really should check on the outpost, I gently remove myself from underneath her sleeping frame. Even as she thrashed, she clung to me like I was the only thing keeping her from sinking into the dark abyss. A lifeline. Like she knew that I would follow her into any darkness just to claw us both back into the light. And I would. Every damn time.

With a quick look over my shoulder, I leave Ramsey in bed and head out in search of food. She has refused every meal that I have offered her, telling me that she is not hungry. But her stomach has been growling in her sleep. She needs fuel in order to regain her magic and strength. It is near dinner time when I make my way into the center of the outpost.

One of the buildings that suffered the most damage is the central kitchen and dining area. Entire walls will need to be replaced. Furniture will need to be mended. But wolves, especially those that live in remote outposts such as this, adapt. Temporary stations have been set up for food prep and cooking near the central fire. The trap that was set in the supply building has been cleaned up, giving access to whatever food stores and tools that remained.

"Is Ramsey okay?" Briar runs up to me as soon as she sees me emerge.

"She will be. She is shaken. Exhausted. The attack seems to have brought back some of her demons." I know that Ramsey has been open with Briar about her past experiences.

"I am proud of her. I wish to see her to tell her myself, but I know that she needs time. What she did…it is not something that many wolves would have the courage to do."

"She is the strongest person I have ever known. Thank you for teaching her how to use those daggers. It saved her life last night. I…I will forever be in your debt." I mean it wholeheartedly.

"You do not owe me anything. I am just thankful that she is okay."

Shifting focus to the rest of the camp, I ask, "How are the injuries? Is anyone in need of help?"

"Everyone is a little beat up, but we will heal. It could have been so much worse."

"And the bodies?"

"Returned to The Mother."

I nod, grateful that the outpost has been mostly cleaned up already. The stench of blood and death are still in the air but that will fade with time.

I make my way over to where we have the temporary kitchen set up and start putting food on a tray for Ramsey, noticing Jovan as he nears.

"Get any sleep?" I ask. His eyes tell me that he slept about as well as I did.

"We all crashed out for a bit. Xylia stayed with us and helped with the pups. Indi needed rest more than we did."

"Will you all be okay here? You are welcome to come to the village once you are up for traveling," I offer.

"We will keep that in mind, but I think we will stay here. It sounds like Koa, the female panther, might be joining our outpost to stay with Reyes. She does not think that he will be welcomed by her family in her territory. I can use her help in defending and hunting."

"She is more than welcome to stay with the pack," I tell him.

I check in with everyone else as I wind through the camp. Ramsey is still asleep when I return so I clean out the tub and request more water to be heated. She will want to take another bath before we head out tomorrow. As long as she is up for it, I plan to run hard so that we make it back to the lodge in three days. Ramsey will benefit from being around her family—our family—while she continues to process the events of last night.

While she sleeps, I reach out to my brothers to update them. *We were attacked last night at an outpost near the border of Nightfury and the panthers. Dreena and many of her followers have been killed.*

"What happened? Is everyone okay? Ramsey?" War asks almost immediately.

"We were attacked during the night. Luckily, Jovan was here and we had five Nightfury soldiers with us. Ramsey was aiding Jovan's Mate in a twin birth. Dreena attacked her while we were distracted by the ambush. Ramsey killed her."

"Fuck." No kidding, War.

"How many casualties?" Bade asks. Due to his headaches, he limits his mind-to-mind contact with us, but this matter is important enough to risk it.

"None from our side. There were 42 including Dreena from her side. We would not have all made it if we did not have the warriors that we did. And a panther shifter fought with us because her Mate is one of the young wolves at the outpost."

"There were almost triple that amount at Dreena's camp where I found Reese. Many of those that attacked you probably escaped with her when my focus switched to a rescue mission. There are more out there. Stay vigilant. She was not working alone."

"Dreena meeting her end is a good thing. She caused too many issues for all of us. Be careful, brothers. We may have removed the original threat, but this battle is not over yet," War advises.

"We should be back to the lodge in a couple of days, as long as Ramsey is up for traveling. She needs her sisters."

"Reese and I will be there soon too. We had to reroute through Nightfang to pick something up on our way home."

We say our goodbyes right as Ramsey shoots straight up in bed, gasping for air. I rushed over to her, pulling her into my arms.

"Are you okay, Angel? Did you have a bad dream?" Her body shakes in my arms as her eyes fill with tears.

"There was so much blood." Her voice shakes as she works to get her words out. "I couldn't figure out where it was coming from but then I looked down and saw that it was coming from me. Dreena was standing over my body smiling down on me as she used a dagger to slice into me over and over."

I hold her a little tighter as she tells me about her nightmare. Ramsey is staring across the room, as if she is seeing something that is not really there.

"And then it shifted. It was me standing over *her* body, just like what actually happened, but it was Ro who was laying behind me. Ro was bleeding so much but I couldn't heal her because I didn't have any magic. There was so much blood. It felt so real. I... I can still smell it."

"That is not going to happen, Angel." I cup her face with my hands. "Rowan is going to be okay. We will make sure of it. And Reese and Bade should be arriving at the lodge close to when we will be back. You and your sisters will all be together again."

Hearing about Reese pulls her out of her negative thoughts. "Did you hear from Bade? What did he say?"

"I was giving an update to both of my brothers right before you woke up. Bade said that they will be at the lodge in a few days. They are in Nightfang right now."

"Did he say anything else? How is Reese doing?"

"He did not say. But she is safe with him. Bade does not talk mind to mind with us often because it causes him headaches—much worse than War or I get."

"Reese gets headaches too," she tells me. "She was on medication for them back in New York. Do you think that is why Zuri and Dreena said that she was sick? Or is it something else? What if...what if she was hurt like I was?"

I do not know what Reese had experienced prior to Bade finding her, but I do know the condition that she was in at that time. Originally, I did not share details with Ramsey because it was not safe for us to travel to her, and I know that she would have insisted, but maybe the details now will help bring her some amount of comfort. Ramsey does better when she knows the facts.

"When Bade found her, Reese was malnourished and weak. She was being held prisoner by Dreena, and she had sores from being chained."

Ramsey sucks in a breath as she listens to me. "But she is okay now?"

"Yes. Bade gave her the rest and nutrition that she needed. I do not know anything else. He has not shared many details of their time together."

We slip into silence while we are both lost in thought. After a while, Ramsey asks, "Do you think that they are True Mates too? Bade would have said something, right?"

"I am not sure if he would." I am hesitant to elaborate, because I do not want her to form any negative feelings toward Bade, but I also do not want to lie to her. "Whether they are Mates or not, Bade will protect her with his life." That I know for certain. "He would do that just because she is your sister. But, I do not know how Bade would handle having a Mate. To my knowledge, he has never wanted one. He saw how devastating it was for our father when our mother died. Out of the three of us, her death affected him the most. Our father had trouble being around him for some time because he looks so much like her in his wolf form. He did not intentionally treat Bade differently, but it happened anyway. Bade has said many times that he would not look for his Mate."

"So, would he reject her? Is that even possible?" I can hear how worried she is for her sister, protective fire burning alongside her words.

"No," I say as I rub small circles on her back. "His wolf would not allow him to. And I think that, with time, he will realize how wonderful it is. If they are Mates, their journey will surely look different from ours."

"Can't you just ask him?" She looks up at me through her eyelashes. ·

I shake my head. "He would have told us if he was ready to. Bade is incredibly private—well, about everything other than sex. I am guessing you do not want me to ask him about his sex life and if it involves your sister."

She snorts. "I'll pass. Though unless she has drastically changed, I'm not sure that she has gotten to know him in that way."

Loving the smile that I put on her face, I decided to try for a laugh. "Maybe we could gift them a butt plug—help them get to know each other really well." I am rewarded with a full laugh and a mischievous smile.

After we eat some food and bathe, Ramsey and I pack up our few belongings and then crawl back into bed. We are planning to leave before the sun tomorrow. It will be nice to be home.

Chapter Twenty-Four

Ramsey

"Holy fuck, Ro! Did you swallow a melon? I was gone for less than two weeks!" I try to hide my laugh as she waddles towards me.

"Just what every girl wants to hear, Rams."

Ro and I squeeze each other tight. Griffin must be exhausted from running us home, but we were able to make it back in two days. We did not pass through any outposts on our way back and only stopped for short meals and periods of rest. I waved goodbye to our travel companions once we got close to the village. They were all grateful to be returning home as well. Briar, Bree, Ebony, Idra, and Tane all promised to keep our lessons going. I thought that my sisters might want to learn too—well, after Rowan has her babies.

"I mean, you look great! Can hardly tell that you are growing multiple babies in your very not large stomach."

Ro snorts. "Nice save. War thinks that it is about half cobbler. But what is the point in having swollen ankles if I can't kick them up and have dessert any time I want?"

"That's the spirit!" I hold my hands to her belly, needing to feel the baby kicks to reassure me that everyone is okay.

"So...how was the trip? You know, other than the whole getting-attacked-and-killing-the-enemy-while-you-saved-a-laboring-mother-and-yourself?"

"Heard about that, huh? Well, other than that, which I still have not fully processed, the trip was really good. It was nice getting to see the world outside the lodge, you know? I was so afraid before, and I still am sometimes, but it was nice to see that I could make it through even if I was nervous."

"And things with you and Griff seem to be going well?"

"We are great. He is my everything."

"It is good to see you happy again." Ro pulls me into another hug, and I can hear her sniffle. I am about to ask if she is okay when she says, "This is why I need cobbler! If I am going to cry at everything, I deserve all of the dessert."

I chuckle into her hair as I hold on to her for longer than normal. She doesn't say anything. She knows that I need this. Soon, she will have three babies to hold on to, but Rowan and Reese were always *my* babies. As fucked up as our childhood was, my relationship with my sisters has always been a bright spot for me. They are mine and they always will be. I have been taking care of them since I was six years old.

"How about we grab some cobbler from the kitchen, and you can tell me about all that I missed when I was away?"

"That sounds perfect. I do need your medical knowledge to help settle a bet that I have with War." I laugh as I follow her into the kitchen. Ro and War are both incredibly competitive. I take a full pan of cobbler out of the fridge while Ro grabs two forks. Apparently, plates are not needed. "Is it my pregnancy hormones that have turned me into a complete horndog or is it my 'incredibly attractive Mate with his giant penis.'" She uses air quotes and a lower voice while giving the second option. Clearly that is War's take.

"Both."

"But you have to pick one!"

"Ro, when two people love each other very much, and one of those people is incredibly attractive with a giant penis…"

"They get pregnant with triplet wolf shifters and need to fuck at least 4 times per day to keep up with the pregnancy hormones?"

"I think you can blame two times on the hormones and the other two on the giant penis," I say. "Professionally speaking, of course."

"And what is your excuse? Personally speaking, of course."

"Oh, I am just a straight up horndog for my hunky wolf man. All of the time. No pregnancy hormones needed."

Griffin and War walk in right then, and the smiles on their faces show me that they both heard that conversation. I wink at Griffin as Ro laughs so hard, she almost pees.

"Busted."

Griffin grabs my fork and tries to eat a bite of cobbler but Ro growls at him like the wolf mama she is. That makes us all laugh. It is so good to be home.

I wrap my arms around Griffin's waist, pulling him close. He gives me a long, slow kiss in greeting. I pull away when I remember that we are not alone.

"Why was that so hot?" Ro says, mouth full of cobbler.

"Hormones," Griffin and I say at the same time.

"Yes! I think that means I won the bet! You better pay up Big Guy," she says to War.

"I already told you that spending an hour between your thighs is no hardship. I need to give my cock a moment of rest anyway," he replies right as Lycus walks into the kitchen.

"Is no place safe?" Lycus mutters as he immediately turns around and leaves the room.

"Father, wait!" Griffin calls out to him, laughing. Lycus returns. "There was an actual reason I wanted to see you. And this is for all of us, so I might as well share it now. I found the passage I was looking for."

We all stare at him, waiting for him to explain further.

"The passage from The Mother that I remembered reading. I was looking in the wrong place. It was in

Mother's last journal. I do not know which text she pulled it from, but it was near the end of her journal, circled multiple times. I think she was trying to find a solution to the losses the pack was already experiencing."

"She was," Lycus confirms. "During her pregnancy with the twins, we had already seen many losses within the pack. She was worried. We had not planned that pregnancy. We were drinking the tea, but she fell pregnant anyway. She was so worried that she would lose the babies. Most losses during those early years were those of the pups and not the mothers."

Griffin passes the journal over to his father. Lycus holds it so gently, running his fingers over her writing, that I can see the love and devastation that he still feels.

"I have not been able to read this journal," he admits. Griffin helps him flip to the correct page and then lets him read it.

And there were <u>Three</u>
Goddesses of The Moon
Born among Man
Awakened by Love
To Bear, Mend, and Find
To Restore the Balance
To Replenish The Mother
Divided, together once more
Hearts will Bind

"She underlined Three," Lycus tells us. "She was thinking of you boys. She was certain that the three of you being Alphas was significant."

"But triplets happen, right? Weren't all pregnancies multiples back then?" Ro asks.

"Triplets did happen but were not as common as twins," Griffin explained.

"And it is very uncommon for more than one alpha to be born in a sibling group," War continued.

"Yes, and when the three of you were all designated as alphas, we knew that you were special. You were born to lead together," Lycus adds.

"But we aren't goddesses. We are human," I say.

"You are a goddess," Griffin replies, "but I think that it is referring to you being Moon Touched."

"Well, I bear," Ro says, pointing to her stomach. "And you mend," she points to me. "Does that mean Reese finds?"

"I think so," Reese's quiet voice says as she enters the kitchen followed by a large Viking of a man that I assume is Bade.

"Reese!" Ro and I both shout as we rush over to her, forcing her into an awkward three-person hug that we have perfected over the years. After several minutes of crying, we pull ourselves apart. It is then that I notice a young child had followed Bade and Reese into the room.

Reese picks up the child. "This is Juniper," she introduces. "She is mine."

After a moment of silent confusion, I ask the question that is probably on everyone's mind. "How is that possible? It has only been a few months since we last saw you."

I step forward, reaching out to tuck some of her wild hair back from her face. "Moon Touched," I whisper as I see the moon markings on her temples. Ro steps closer, lowering her neckline to show her moon markings while I lift my hands.

Noticing the Moon Touched markings that adorn her temples, we all are momentarily struck speechless. How is it possible that being Moon Touched is almost unheard of—yet we have all been blessed? It really just reaffirms my belief that my sisters and I were born in the wrong world. We were always meant to be here.

"And there were three, goddesses of the moon," Griffin says.

"Are you mated?" War asks.

Reese and Bade both sharply say no, leaving us all wondering what the story is there. There is clearly tension between them, though they seem comfortable enough around each other.

Ro directs the conversation back to Reese and Juniper, asking again how it is possible. It looks like Reese is about to explain when we are interrupted by another male entering the kitchen.

"Sylas?" Ro growls, War moving to her side as his wolf tears through his skin.

Not sure what is happening, I move myself back into the safety of Griffin's arms.

"What is he doing here?" Ro snarls, as War's wolf lets out a low warning growl.

Griffin shifts me behind him. "How could you bring him here?" he asks Bade.

After some more back and forth, it is decided that Reese and Bade will explain why Sylas is here, but only after he removes himself from the lodge.

Lycus talks War into shifting back and we all move into the living room where we can be a little more comfortable. Still feeling shaken by the whole event, I sit down on Griffin's lap, needing his comfort, as we settle in for Reese's story.

Chapter Twenty-Five

We spent most of the night catching up with Reese and Bade. I am still processing most of what they told us as Griffin and I crawl into our bed for the first time in a couple of weeks. I sigh as my body is enveloped in the familiar comfort and scent of us.

"It is so nice to be back home," I yawn as Griffin tucks my body against him.

"How are you feeling?" Griffin places a tender kiss on my collar bone as he slowly massages my sore muscles.

"I am feeling so many things. I am thankful that Reese is finally home with us and that Ro and her babies are healthy. I am saddened by all of the lives that have been lost just because of someone's greed for power. I feel safe and settled, like you are the home I have always searched for. The only one that I have ever needed."

Griffin continues kissing a path down my body. "What else are you feeling, Angel?"

"I feel loved." My words turn raspy as my body begins to heat under his ministrations. "So loved that it might burst out of my skin."

"That sounds serious." He has completely given up on my massage and is now scraping his teeth and flicking his tongue all over my body.

"It is," I moan.

"You are shaking, pretty girl. Maybe we should do something to relieve some of that pressure before you blow like a gasket."

He pulls my nipple into his mouth as his hand snakes down between my legs. I widen my legs for him, unashamed of how wet he is going to find me.

"I'm open to suggestions." I bite my bottom lip as he drags a knuckle through my center.

"What do you think would be most effective? My hand, my mouth, or my cock?" He gives me a little preview of each before adding, "for science."

I push him onto his back so that I can climb up and straddle him. "Well, if it is for science, we should probably try all three." I flip myself around, hovering my dripping pussy over his gorgeous face, giving him a front row seat to my most intimate areas. Griffin growls and then spanks my ass, making my walls squeeze around nothing.

"Tongue first." He yanks me to his mouth, spearing his tongue into me as his finger rubs circles over my clit. I am already so worked up, it will not take me long to fall over the edge.

But I want him to come with me. Gripping his cock in my hands, I lower my mouth to his head, licking the precum that is already leaking from him. Taking him further into my mouth, I swirl my tongue around his shaft just how he likes it. Reaching back to add my own fingers into my pussy, I get them nice and wet before pressing them against Griffin's asshole.

"Now be a good boy and make me come while I choke on your cock."

He bucks up into my mouth as my finger enters him, his moans vibrate against my pussy lips before he sucks my clit into his mouth.

"Fuck!" His shout fills my mind, echoing my own thoughts as we both shatter, bodies convulsing, my grip on his knot remaining firm even as the rest of my body collapses on top of him.

I'm not sure how long we stay like that. I might even fall asleep for a short time because the next thing that I know, my body is airborne.

"Griff, do you—" Lycus's voice is not one that I was expecting to hear as I crash down onto the floor.

"Father!" Griffin yells. "Fuck, sorry Angel."

I peek over the edge of the bed, my body mostly hidden by the mattress as Griffin springs into action, grabbing a blanket to wrap around me and pull me to standing.

Lycus's eyes are as big as saucers, a deer stuck in headlights, as he tries to process the image that he just walked in on.

Mortified, my cheeks turn beet red to match the blush that has colored his face as well. There is no way that he did not see my ass, and probably more, as I was star-fished across his son after one of the most powerful orgasms of my life. Griffin's cock was still in my hand!

Nobody is saying anything. We are all just staring at each other until I offer an awkward wave, unsure what to do with my hands.

Griffin snorts at the motion. "Father, was there something that you needed?" Finally finding some words to string together into a sentence.

"I…uh…Well, I was just coming to see if you had more of your Mother's journals. War told me that you were still up reading."

"Those shit-stirrers." I laugh. "We are going to have to get them back for this." There is no doubt in my mind that Ro is equally as responsible for this interruption.

Leaving me laughing in my blanket cocoon, Griffin walks over to the fireplace and removes a stack of journals from the bookshelf. He winks at me before handing them to his father and ushering him to the door. "If that is all, Father, Ramsey and I have at least two more scientific experiments to conduct tonight."

Lycus leaves the room mumbling something that sounded like, "It's always the quiet ones," as he shakes his head.

"I can't believe he just saw my ass," I whisper-shout to Griffin as he pulls me back into bed.

He laughs hard. "It could have been worse."

"How could it possibly have been worse than him seeing my bare ass as I am holding your cock and am passed out from the force of the orgasm that you just gave me?"

"He could have walked in on me filling your ass—which I definitely plan on doing tonight, by the way. For science."

I giggle. "Well, of course. For science." I bring my lips to his, devouring his mouth with my own as our bodies become reacquainted with each other. "Is there anything else you would like to try tonight? For science?"

"Everything, Angel. I want everything with you."

"You can have it," I whisper against his lips. "Everything that I am is yours. It always has been. From the very start. Even when I couldn't recognize myself—I was yours."

Griffin slides into me, his thrusts slow but firm as my entire body lights up with love for him.

"Thank you for bringing me home, Griffin."

"Always."

Chapter Twenty-Six

Ramsey

(18 Months Later)

I have felt off all day. Moving from one appointment to the other, I am thankful that Heka moved all of my patients to appointments at the lodge, no longer wanting me to travel around the city in my later stages of pregnancy. According to how I am progressing, I still have about a month to go before my babies will be ready to be born, but growing three babies has made it more difficult to move around.

I miss Griffin. He left yesterday morning to attend to some issues at an outpost and will not be returning until tonight. He was not going to leave me for that long, but I convinced him that he needed to. It is better that he makes the rounds at some of his outposts now before we have our hands full with triplets.

Feeling sweaty and sore from the day, I run myself a cool bath, hoping that the water will relieve some of the weight of my belly from my back. Once I am in the water, I run my hands over my stomach, letting my magic travel within myself.

I only allow myself to check like this once per week—just like how a doctor would schedule an appointment weekly at this stage in my pregnancy. If I used my magic more than that, I would probably become obsessive about every little thing. So, once per week, I give myself an ultrasound.

Just as I am about to open my magical inner mind, Juni comes rushing into my bathroom, looking worried. That is when I feel it. A gush of fluid.

Juni comes over and holds my hand, worry fills her eyes as she looks towards the door.

"Ro, Reese—I need you in my bathroom right now!"

"Already on my way!" Reese tells me.

"I'll be there in two minutes. Are you okay?"

"I am pretty sure my water just broke. It's too early. Griffin isn't here. Juni is."

Looking down, I see that my body is mostly covered by the bubbles that I added to my bath. "Bade!" I shout. "You can come in. I'm in the bath."

Almost instantly, Bade walks into the room, walking straight over to Juni. "Griff is on his way home. He will be here in a couple of hours."

"It is too early. They aren't ready yet." I can't keep the panic out of my voice.

"You can make them ready." Juni's voice is quiet as she clings to my hand. "Use your magic and make them ready."

My eyes shift from Juni to Bade and back to Juni. "I have never done that before."

Bade looks down at Juni, seeming to have a conversation with her without words. Nodding, he looks back over to me.

"You can do it," he tells me firmly.

Bade takes Juni's hand and leaves the room as my sisters run through the door.

"I've got the bed!" Reese shouts from my bedroom.

"Hey, Rams," Ro says as she approaches the bathtub. "Where are we at in the process?"

"It's too early. They aren't ready."

261

"They will be okay. If your water broke, then they are eager to make their entrance." She is using the same words that I have told countless mothers over the years, but they do little to ease my worry.

"They aren't ready," I say again. "I need to check them. I need to make sure that their lungs are developed enough. If their lungs aren't ready, they won't be able to breathe. If they can't breathe, then they will die. I will not let that happen."

"Then use your magic to check. You can do this, Ramsey." Reese says as she joins us in the bathroom.

"They need to keep growing. They need to stay in my belly where they are safe. Griffin isn't even home right now. It isn't time."

"Sometimes they make different plans, Rams. But you can check. Use your magic to check."

Nodding, I wipe the tears from my cheeks and put my hands back on my bump. Focusing my attention on one baby at a time, I check on their development.

Baby A, Emma, is our blondie. She has a full head of hair, all of her fingers and toes, and is right on track to be born in around four more weeks. She will need help developing her lungs before I let her out of my belly. She has always been the one who moves the most. Wild from the very start. Before I help her out, I look at her sisters.

Baby B, Esme, is our redhead. Smaller than the others, her movements have always been gentle—quiet—but no less present. Her lungs and eyes will need a boost before I let her out into the world.

Baby C, Eloise, my mini-me. She will need to be a fighter. In addition to her lungs and eyes needing more time, her heartbeat has slowed. She is in distress and needs help now.

Keeping some of my magic wrapped around the other two, I focus my attention on Eloise, helping her lungs and eyes develop to how they should be at time of delivery. With her heart, I find a small hole, which I patch up before giving her entire body an extra boost of my magic.

"What's going on, Ramsey?" Ro's voice cuts through my concentration.

"They aren't ready. I just helped Eloise. I need to help the others too."

"You are sweating. Be careful." I can hear the concern in Reese's voice, but know that I will not stop until all three of my babies are safe. She knows it too.

Esme is next. Her lungs and eyes are the most underdeveloped of the three. I pour my magic into her tiny body, encouraging the growth that she needs.

"Ramsey." I can feel Reese's hand on my shoulder as she shakes me. Opening my eyes, her face slowly comes into focus. "Are you okay?"

Panting, I nod my head.

"You should take a break," Ro suggests. "It has been over an hour since you started. Let us check you."

It has been over an hour? It feels like only minutes have passed. My contractions are strong—painful—but I do my best to block them out. These babies will not be delivered until they are strong enough.

Shaking my head at my sisters, I gulp down the water that they offer and then focus my magic once more. Emma. My wild child. She will need working lungs in order to cause all of the mischief that I know she is destined to create. I can feel my magic depleting. I will not have much left after I have helped them all—but that is okay. They just need to be healthy. That is what matters.

Pushing every last bit of my magic that I can manage into my girls, I release my hold and let my head drop back. Exhausted.

I'm not sure how much time has passed, but the next thing I know, Griffin's arms are circling around me as he pulls me out of the cool water.

"I'm here, Angel. You are going to be okay."

"I made them ready." My words are no more than a mumble as my body slowly drifts back into awareness. Breathing hard, I yell as a strong contraction wakes me further.

"She is fully dilated, Griff." Ro's voice shakes me awake.

Looking around the room, I see my sisters and my Mate, looking at me with equal parts concern and wonder.

"They are ready. I made them ready." Griffin kisses me, holding his hand to my belly as tears run down his face.

"Are *you* ready?" He asks. Always putting me first.

I nod. Wanting nothing more than to hold my babies in my arms.

Emma is born first. No surprise there. Of course she would want to lead her sisters into this crazy world.

Next is Eloise. Fighting for that second spot. She struggles a bit at first, but once she sorts herself out, she joins us sunny side up.

Finally, Esme makes her entrance. Small and quiet, but she holds our attention with her expressive eyes.

All three babies were born a month too soon. All three babies were born completely healthy thanks to the magic that I was blessed with. I have never been more grateful to have this magic than I am right now.

My vision is blurry as I try to focus on the movements throughout the room. War and Bade have come into the room, helping Reese with my babies while Rowan and Griff stay with me.

Hearing a catch in her breath, I lock eyes with Ro and instantly know that something is wrong. Sniffing the air, I know what it is. Blood.

"What is happening, Ro?"

"It's going to be okay. There is just some bleeding. War, can you bring me some of those towels and some clean water?"

"How much bleeding?" I look over to Griffin who has the same panic on his face that I feel inside. "How much bleeding?"

"I think you have a tear, Ramsey. Can you use your magic? Find the tear?"

I try. I really, really, try. But my well has been depleted. I used it all to save the babies. "I can't. There isn't any left."

Griffin chokes out a sob before bringing my hand up to his mouth. "Please, Angel. Please heal yourself. I need you to be okay."

"I love you," I tell him.

"I love you too. But you need to heal. This is not the end, Angel."

"It was always a risk. But you were worth every minute of it."

"You are going to be okay. I need you to be okay. You have survived worse."

I nod my head as I feel my energy leaving my body.

"I'm going to slow the bleeding, Ramsey." I can feel Ro pushing her magic into me, trying to help even though her magic does not work that way. "Please." She begs. "Let me save you. You saved me."

Griffin reaches down to grab my hand. "I would do it all again. Every moment. I would do it all again. But I need you to fight, Angel. You are so strong. You can fight this."

I look around the room and see my family. My sisters, their Mates, my Mate, my babies. "I need to hold my babies."

Reese and Bade rush over to me, placing my babies on my chest. Their little warm bodies squirm against my cold skin. "I have loved you from the beginning."

The sounds of heartbreak being ripped from Griffin's chest are the last that I hear before the world goes dark.

Chapter Twenty-Seven

Griffin

"Heal. Please, Angel. I need you to heal." Ramsey's body turns colder by the minute, the blood loss too fast for her body to keep up with.

I bury my head in her neck, laying a protective arm around my Mate as she holds our babies to her chest.

"Please, love. I need you in this world with me. I cannot do this without you."

Her breaths are so labored, they rattle as she pulls the little bit of air that she can manage into her lungs to breathe. I can feel her heart slowing beneath me.

I growl as I feel a hand touch my arm. "Let me take the babies, Griffin." Reese's voice is calm despite the anguish I know she feels. "Let me hold them while you hold her."

"No!" I roar. It is taking too much concentration to not shift into my wolf right now and rip the entire world apart. Ramsey would not want me to do that. She would want me to hold her. "She wanted to hold them. I just... I need to let her hold them."

Reese retreats back into Bade's arms. I will apologize to her later. After Ramsey gets better.

I look over and see War holding Rowan as she almost collapses to the floor, covered in Ramsey's blood. "It's not working. I tried, but my power can't mend. I couldn't..."

Turning back to my Mate, I close my eyes and bring my lips to her ear. I tell her how much I love her. I remind her of her strength. I try to force any healing powers that I have through our bond, hoping that I can stem the bleeding long enough for her own healing to kick in. I tell her how beautiful our daughters are. So small but so perfect. Looking like mini versions of her and her sisters—just like she told me they would. Over and over again, I repeat my vows to her. The words that we shared under the moon flow off of my tongue as a promise and a reminder of how much she is needed here. How much her sisters and our babies and me...how much I need her here.

My eyes are closed but a flash of silver moonlight causes me to open them. Looking down at her chest, bright silver light flows through her body. Reese and Ramsey gasp as they step closer.

"Her power is coming back!" Rowan puts words to the thoughts that I have running through my head. She is doing it. She is healing herself.

"It isn't her." Reese points to the three little glow worms wriggling on Ramsey's chest. "The babies are healing her."

"How is that possible?" Afraid that it will make them stop if I move, I keep my arm draped over them, holding them securely to their mother's chest.

After a few minutes, the glow begins to recede. The babies all start crying, clearly affected by the power that they just used. The room is silent as we all count Ramsey's breaths—waiting for her to wake.

One.

Two.

Three.

Four.

Gasping, Ramsey sits up, quickly bringing her arm up to help support the babies as I remain paralyzed by shock.

"What happened?" Her voice is raspy—but it is the best sound I have ever heard. Sobs wrack my body as I climb further onto the bed and pull my family into my arms.

"The babies," Reese tells her. "The babies healed you."

Ramsey looks down at our daughters, now sleeping peacefully in our arms. "What do you mean?"

"They went full glow worm. You...you lost too much blood. Your heart stopped. I heard it happen." Rowan shakes her head, unable to believe what we all just saw happen. "But they healed you."

"They have magic? Are they Moon Touched?"

"I do not know, Angel. It was like when you saved Rowan. But they do not have markings on their hands. Look."

She looks down at our perfect little girls. Not a single shimmery mark on them.

"Can all of the babies use our magic? Can all of our Moon Touched magic be passed down?"

"I do not know, sweetheart."

"Will their magic come back?" She looks down at our sleeping girls, so brave and strong on their first day of life.

"I do not know." I tell her, again.

"What does it mean?"

The first time that I saw Ramsey, she was standing in a pool of blood, terrified of my brother but desperate to save her sister's life. Moon Touched magic, True Mate bonds, humans being brought to this world—at that time we did not know what any of it meant. But we figured it out. Just like we will figure this out too. So, what does this mean? Easy.

"It means that I am the luckiest guy in the world."

Author's Note

Thank you for reading the second installment of The Moon Touched Chronicles. The fact that you took the time to read words that I put down on a page means more to me than you will ever know.

I created the FMCs in this series years ago—long before the idea of pairing them up with wolf shifters ever occurred to me. Just like how I was confident that Rowan needed to be the sister who opened the series—I knew that Ramsey was destined to share a story of incredible strength. It was written into her DNA from the very start.

While their connection was fated, Ramsey and Griffin built their relationship on friendship and trust. I can picture this couple cozying up with a book, sharing deep intellectual conversation, and, of course, conducting as many science experiments as possible.

Griffin and Ramsey may have received their happily ever after, but you do not need to say goodbye just yet. Rowan, War, Ramsey, and Griffin will be making frequent appearances as the story concludes in Reese and Bade's book, Nightfury.

Keep reading for a sneak peek at *Nightfury.*

Content Warning

This book contains strong language, sexually explicit scenes, discussions of drink tampering, violence, kidnapping, child neglect, poisoning, societal infertility, pregnancy, childbirth, and loss.

The Moon Touched Chronicles

Nightfang

Nighthowl

Nightfury

The Sun Kissed Scrolls

Lightclaw

(Coming Soon)

<u>www.rubyellisauthor.com</u>

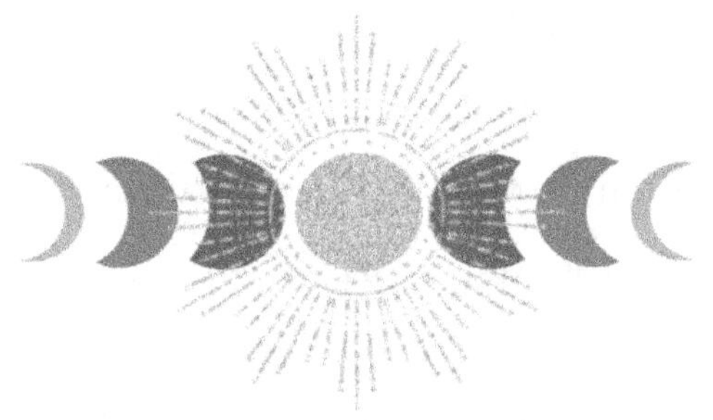

Chapter One

"This is Juniper," I explained. "She is mine."

I had planned so many different ways to tell my sisters about Juni but walking into the kitchen—seeing them for the first time in months—I completely forgot the thought-out introduction that I was going to use and instead uttered a simple, 'she is mine.' I mentally face-palm and tack on a smile in hopes that this isn't as awkward as it seems. But it is. I know that it is. Because we are standing in a kitchen, surrounded by people who were definitely not expecting us to waltz in with a child, and not a single breath can be heard. Not even my own. The air has been completely sucked out of the room until Ramsey breaks the silence.

"How is that possible? It has only been a few months since we last saw you." Her confusion is completely understandable. But I still have not regained control over my tongue. Words are impossible right now.

Standing next to Ramsey is a large man with short, brown hair and piercing blue eyes. He looks at her like she has hung the moon.

She steps closer and tucks a strand of my wild hair behind my ear. That is when she notices the markings on my temple. She looks at the little girl in my arms and then turns to Bade. She sucks in a sharp breath as she notices the matching marks on his face.

"Moon Touched." Her words are barely more than a whisper. Revered.

Ramsey shows me the marks on her hands while Rowan steps forward and pulls the neckline of her dress down. She has the marks too. Taking a closer look at the men who must be Bade's brothers, Warrick and Griffin, I see that they have matching markings with my sisters.

"And there were three, goddesses of the moon," the brother whose marks match Ramsey says.

"Are you Mated?" the other brother asks. His marks match Rowan's. He is just as tall as Bade, with shoulder length black hair and blue eyes that match both brothers.

There is another man in the room who looks slightly older, though it is hard to tell with their extended lifespans. His eyes are green, but he has dark features like Ro's Mate.

"No," Bade and I answered at the same time. It comes out a little harsher than I mean, but it is the truth all the same. Bade and I have come a long way to be where we are right now, but we still have further to go on our journey towards whatever we will be.

"We will revisit that later," Rowan says. "Can someone please explain how this adorable little girl is yours? I got knocked up almost immediately after we arrived in this world and my babies are still cooking."

I look down at Ro's swollen belly. She looks like she could be due any day, though admittedly, I do not know much about wolf-shifter gestation.

I am about to speak when Sylas enters the kitchen. Bade told him to wait outside the lodge but his wolf did not want Juni to meet new, powerful people without him present. Bade assured him that she would not be in any danger here, but he had to see for himself. I rolled my eyes as they argued about it on our way here. There are still a lot of things about this world that I do not understand, and the complexities of sharing souls is one of them.

Upon seeing Sylas, the mood in the room changes drastically. All of the warmth I felt when reuniting with my sisters has cooled down to freezing. It is clear that Sylas is not welcome. Ramsey retreats into her Mate's arms while Rowan's Mate shifts into a massive black wolf, positioning himself between Sylas and everyone else.

Apparently, there was cause for concern with this meeting after all—though it seems to have nothing to do with Juni and *everything* to do with Sylas.

"What is he doing here?" Rowan snarls so fiercely that she seems more wolf than human. Bade's brothers must have done that mind communication thing because Ramsey is pulled behind her Mate while a fierce growl leaves his chest.

I look to Sylas, unsure as to what is happening right now. He does not give me any indication that he understands what this is about either. Bade moves so that he is in front of me and Juni, leaving Sylas to stand on his own while he faces more than one angry Alpha.

"How could you bring him here?" Ramsey's Mate asks Bade.

"You need to allow Reese to explain, Griff," Bade replies.

"Reese is welcome to explain, but Sylas needs to leave the lodge right the fuck now," Griffin replies. "War is barely able to hold himself back." War, the wolf, is growling and pacing in front of Ro. She reaches down to touch his back but the look on her face is almost as menacing.

"Why?" I ask quietly. I have no idea what would cause such a strong reaction. I didn't even know that they knew Sylas.

"Because his chosen mate almost killed me and my unborn children a few weeks ago," Rowan says. "He needs to leave before War rips his throat out."

Sylas's face turns white as he steps back to stand in the doorway. "I did not know," he tells them. "I did not know."

"Go wait outside," Bade tells him. Sylas nods his head and backs out of the kitchen. Nobody moves until we hear the front door snick closed.

"Perhaps we should move somewhere more comfortable?" the older man suggests. "War, shift back so that we can figure this out. Your Mate and pups are safe with all of us here."

War shifts back into his human form and moves to stand behind Rowan, pulling her flush against his body. Griffin opens a cabinet and pulls out a pair of pants for War to put on.

"We keep pants in the kitchen now?" The corner of Bade's mouth hitches up in half a smile.

"I started stashing them around the lodge when Rowan moved in. I do not need her seeing your cocks all of the time," War replies.

"Jealous, brother?" Bade jokes.

"There is no need to be jealous," Rowan jumps in. "You are all massive. I am far more concerned with a bare ass on the sofa situation."

"And nobody needs to get poked in the eye at the dinner table," Ramsey adds.

I can't help the laugh that bursts out of me. I have missed my sisters so much.

We all move into a room with more comfortable seating. Juni has fallen asleep in my arms so Bade gently pulls her away from me and lays her down on one of the comfortable couches, covering her with a blanket. Everyone in the room tracks the movement but don't say anything.

Unlike how my sisters are pulled down onto their Mates' laps, Bade sits down next to me. A pang of jealousy runs through me at the open displays of possessive affection that are shown to my sisters. I am not even sure if I want the whole 'over possessive mate thing'—my feelings for Bade are complicated—but I am jealous all the same.

Shaking off the feeling, I focus my attention on the familiar faces in the room. "Where should I start?"

"At the beginning," Ramsey replies. "We want to know everything."